The Bard's Daughter

The Gareth and Gwen Medieval Mysteries
(a prequel)

THE BARD'S DAUGHTER

by

SARAH WOODBURY

The Bard's Daughter
Copyright © 2012 by Sarah Woodbury

This is a work of fiction.

To my mom
who loves a good mystery

A Brief Guide to Welsh Pronunciation

c a hard 'c' sound (Cadfael)

ch a non-English sound as in Scottish "ch" in "loch" (Fychan)

dd a buzzy 'th' sound, as in "there" (Ddu; Gwynedd)

f as in "of" (Cadfael)

ff as in "off" (Gruffydd)

g a hard 'g' sound, as in "gas" (Goronwy)

l as in "lamp" (Llywelyn)

ll a breathy /sh/ sound that does not occur in English (Llywelyn)

rh a breathy mix between 'r' and 'rh' that does not occur in English (Rhys)

th a softer sound than for 'dd,' as in "thick" (Arthur)

u a short 'ih' sound (Gruffydd), or a long 'ee' sound (Cymru—pronounced "kumree")

w as a consonant, it's an English 'w' (Llywelyn); as a vowel, an 'oo' sound (Bwlch)

y the only letter in which Welsh is not phonetic. It can be an 'ih' sound, as in "Gwyn," is often an "uh" sound (Cymru), and at the end of the word is an "ee" sound (thus, both Cymru—the modern word for Wales—and Cymry—the word for Wales in the Dark Ages—are pronounced "kumree")

1

Carreg Cennen Castle

January 1141

G wen stopped short when she reached the bottom rung
of the ladder that descended into the pantry. She didn't
want to go on. Out of a childish curiosity which she tried not
to indulge too often, she and her brother, Gwalchmai, had
explored the castle three months ago when they'd first
arrived. This pantry lay at the near end of a hollowed out
cave in the rock that supported Carreg Cennen Castle. It was
little used, being less accessible and too moist compared to
the other storage areas. Gwen touched a hand to the stones
of the wall, feeling the damp beneath her fingers.

Edain, the serving boy who'd come to find her, urged
her onward, waiting for her to step past him. But she
couldn't make her feet move. Two lanterns lit the room and
half a dozen men crowded into it, including Robert, the

castle's steward, Gruffydd, the captain of the garrison, and several of his soldiers.

Her father sat on a low stool before her, his head bent and his hands hanging off his knees. In front of him on the floor lay the sprawled body of Collen, a merchant whom they'd often met on the road, walking from castle to castle and tiny village to tiny village, hawking his wares. Since coins were rare in Wales, he bartered more often than he sold. It was from him that a girl could acquire a new needle or a fine ribbon. Gwen touched the top of her head, tracing the green silken length in her hair that was one of her most prized possessions. She'd gotten it from Collen, quite literally, for a song.

Gwen didn't have to ask if Collen was dead. Blood trickled from underneath his head, staining the uneven stones of the floor around his body. Next to Collen lay one of her father's iron harp strings, as if the murderer, having done his work, had discarded it carelessly on the ground. Red stained the length of it, matching the blood covering her father's hands.

"You must come with me, Meilyr." Gruffydd stood before her father, his fists on his hips. The captain of the guard was tall and distinguished, in his middle thirties, with the thick shoulders and legs of a fighting man. Edain had come for her so quickly that she had arrived on Sir Gruffydd's heels.

Gwen squeezed the boy's arm, hardly able to keep her feet.

"What did you say?" Meilyr peered at Collen's body and then up at Gruffydd. "I don't want to come with you. My friend is dead. I should stay with him."

"Collen is dead by your hand," Gruffydd said.

Meilyr's mouth fell open. "Wh-wh-what?"

Gwen clenched her hands into fists and brought them to her lips. She couldn't take it in. Her father couldn't have murdered Collen. *He couldn't have.* "Please, Sir Gruffydd!" Gwen's voice went high and tears pricked at the corners of her eyes. "My father didn't do this!"

"Does this belong to him?" With the toe of his boot, Gruffydd indicated the bloody harp string.

Gwen swallowed. "Yes, but—"

Gruffydd tucked the fingers of one hand under Meilyr's arm, surprisingly gently given the circumstances, and pulled him up from his stool. Meilyr didn't protest.

Robert clasped his hands behind his back. "I suppose that's that." He headed towards the exit where Gwen stood. When he reached her, he rested a hand her shoulder. "I'm sorry, Gwen."

Gwen nodded dumbly, her attention still on her father. For Meilyr's part, he didn't seem to realize what was happening. Gwen stepped further into the room to let all the men file past her but one guard, who remained leaning against the far wall of the pantry. As her father came abreast of her, she looked directly into his eyes. He brought up one bloody hand to block the light from the lantern which one of the soldiers held high in front of him. In spite of the bright light, his pupils were dilated.

And then as Meilyr passed by without looking at her, Gwen got a whiff of his breath.

"He's drunk," Edain said, with all the tactlessness of a fourteen-year-old boy. "And at this hour of the morning."

A moan rose in Gwen's throat. She wanted to go back in time to the moment Edain had come to find her. He'd stood panting in the doorway of the herbalist's hut, where Gwen and Gwalchmai had been practicing their scales. The hut lay in a far corner of the kitchen garden and had the benefit of being out of the wind, although since it had no windows, they had been working by the light of a low burning brazier and a single candle. It could have been a summer's day at noon and Gwen wouldn't have known it but for the cold and the square of pale light coming through the open doorway, which Edain's slender figure had blocked.

Edain had demanded that she come with him. At the time, she'd stared at him, a denial forming in her throat. She swallowed it down, however, as she swallowed down most of her retorts these days. She was a grown woman and should be beyond petulance.

Gwen turned her head to watch her father go. "Either that, or he drank so much mead last night that it has yet to wear off."

Edain brushed a lock of light brown hair out of his eyes and shrugged. Usually, he was so talkative it was difficult to get in a word between his stories.

In retrospect, Gwen thought her guess more likely than Edain's. Her father had been struggling with drink since her mother died, conquering it for months at a time, only to sink back into despair and begin the cycle anew. Even on his worst days, however, he made an effort not to drink until the sun had set—which was easier in winter, with its short days and long nights.

Gwen rubbed at her temples with her fingers. Her father had been much more in control during this last year, as Gwalchmai's singing voice had begun to manifest. She had actually believed that he'd finally mastered himself for good.

Gruffydd's barking order to find a board so they could get the body out of the pantry echoed from above. Pounding feet indicated that men were obeying him. Gwen stared at her own feet, feeling herself a coward for not protesting more and for allowing Gruffydd to lead her father away.

Gwen pressed her forehead into the cold stones of the wall, her eyes shut tight. "What am I to do, Edain?"

"You really don't think your father did it?" Edain said. "How could you doubt it, given what lies before us?"

"Of course, I doubt it." Gwen tipped her head to look up at Edain. He loomed over her. He'd added two inches to his already lanky frame since Gwen's family had arrived at Carreg Cennen in the autumn, and would probably grow more. "You saw my father. He could barely stand."

"Mead makes some men stronger than when they're sober." Philip, the guard who'd been left behind, straightened from his position against the wall. He was one of Gruffydd's more able and reliable soldiers.

"Even if I admit that my father could have overcome Collen," Gwen said, "it couldn't have been that easy. How could my father have wrapped that string around Collen's throat without Collen fighting back? My father doesn't have a mark on his face or arms."

"Meilyr's hands have Collen's blood on them." Philip said. "You have to prepare yourself, Gwen. If your father is convicted of Collen's murder, you know what comes next."

Gwen gazed down at Collen's body. She did know: shame, mortification, banishment. The fine—*galanas*—that he would owe Collen's family would pauper them. Gwen swallowed down those thoughts. Her father hadn't murdered Collen, and if he hadn't murdered him, then someone else had.

"I would have blood on my hands too if I came upon a friend who lay dead on the floor," Gwen said. "My father touched Collen. He's drunk enough that maybe he thought Collen was asleep at first. That is all."

Neither Philip nor Edain looked convinced. Edain pursed his lips. "I don't know, Gwe—"

Gwalchmai hurtled down the ladder and collided with Gwen, unable to stop his headlong rush. "I saw Gruffydd take Father away!" Gwalchmai wrapped his arms around Gwen's waist. "What's happening? What did he do?"

Gwen's brother was ten years younger than she and developing a soprano voice that her father swore would shake the rafters of every hall in which he sang. To Gwen's ear, it already did. Gwen took in a deep breath, knowing that she had to be strong for him, and then eased back from Gwalchmai enough to bend and put her hands to either side of his face. "Collen is dead. That's all we know so far. I will come find you in a moment."

"Father has been accused of murdering Collen, hasn't he, Gwen? I heard someone in the kitchen say it." Gwalchmai gazed into Gwen's face, eyes wide.

"You and I both know that he couldn't have done anything like that, but it is what Gruffydd and Robert believe," Gwen said.

"What if he did it?" Gwalchmai edged sideways, his eyes flicking all around the room, trying to look past Gwen to Collen's body.

Gwen shifted her body to block his vision. "Gwalchmai! How could you even think such a thing of Father?"

Her brother tried to pull away. "Everyone else is thinking it. How do you know Father is innocent?"

"I just *do*! Regardless, you shouldn't be here."

"But Gwen—"

"Not now, Gwalchmai. Wait for me in the kitchen." Gwen forcibly turned her brother around and marched him towards the ladder.

Gwalchmai's face wore a mutinous look, but he allowed her to shove him up the steps. His feet stomped at each rung in turn until he disappeared and Gwen turned back to the body. She hated seeing the merchant this way, and hated even more that Philip now crouched beside the body.

"Do you—do you see anything that could exonerate my father?" she said.

Philip gestured to Collen's body. "Not from here." He glanced up at her. "It could even be a hanging if Lord Cadfael is in a vindictive mood."

Gwen and her family had spent the winter singing for Lord Cadfael, the ruler of Carreg Cennen. From here, Lord Cadfael oversaw Bychan, a cantref in the Welsh kingdom of Deheubarth, and was himself subject to the oversight of Deheubarth's king, Anarawd.

The lump in Gwen's throat was so big now that she couldn't swallow. Thank goodness Collen lay face down so she couldn't see the wound at his throat. Her eyes teared again as she gazed at him and she was honest enough with herself to admit that the tears were less for Collen than for herself and her family. If this accusation stuck, no man would ever respect her father again. And who would hire the son of a murderer to sing in his hall?

"How long ago did he die?" Edain said.

Philip lifted up Collen's wrist and dropped it. "He's warm but stiff."

"What does that mean?" Edain stepped closer, bending forward with his hands on his knees, all eyes.

"If he were warm but not stiff, Collen would have died within the last few hours. As it is, the stiffness implies that he died sometime after midnight, but before dawn."

Gwen wiped at her cheeks with the back of her hand. She found herself trembling at how casually Edain and Philip discussed Collen's demise.

Edain touched a finger to a spot on Collen's breeches.

"Here! What are you doing?" Philip said.

"That's not blood," Edain said.

"Of course it's blood," Philip said. "There's blood all over him."

This wasn't strictly true. The pantry sloped away from its highest point by the ladder and the blood had poured from Collen's wound towards a far corner, without sullying the floor under the rest of Collen's body. Ignoring Philip, Edain leaned in and sniffed at the stain.

"What is it?" Gwen said.

"It smells somewhat sweet, maybe nutty," Edain said.

Philip snorted in disgust. In a manner similar to the one Gruffydd had used with her father, though perhaps with even more understanding, he took Edain's arm to pull him up and out of his way.

"This is no place for you, boy," Philip said. "For neither you nor Gwen." He turned to her. "You should see to your brother."

"He's right, Gwen," Edain said.

Gwen backed away as two guards awkwardly lowered a body-sized board down the ladder. Philip caught one end and set it on the floor of the pantry. "Excuse us, Gwen," one of the other guards said.

Philip nudged Edain and Gwen. "I know you're curious," he said. "But even if Meilyr isn't guilty, there's nothing you can do about it. Leave this to your betters."

"Yes, sir," Edain said.

Gwen didn't answer, just tugged her cloak tighter around her shoulders, feeling colder than she should have in the protected pantry. She was thankful for her thick woolen leggings and two petticoats that kept the worst of the winter air from freezing her to her bones. Gwen watched the guards lift Collen onto the board and then turned away. There was no going back to a time before Collen's death. A wail rose in her chest.

What am I going to do?

2

Gwen entered the garden, her heart pounding so hard in her ears that she could barely hear the crunch of her footsteps on the gravel of the pathway that led to the herbalist's hut where she could hide. Then she stopped and shut her eyes. After she'd left the pantry, she'd gone to the kitchen to find Gwalchmai as she had promised. She'd told him that no matter what happened, she would take care of him. He needed her now. She had to be strong for him. Taking another deep breath, she turned on her heel and headed for the barracks where Gruffydd had taken her father.

As she approached the door to her father's cell, the guard glared at her as if she, too, had murdered someone. She looked past him, through the barred window. Her father had transferred his slumped posture from the stool in the pantry to a bench against the wall in a cell with a stone floor and walls. The door was locked and guarded, too, and the guard outside admitted Gwen only after she handed over her belt knife.

Gwen came to a halt in front of her father. She didn't know what to say to him and she was afraid that anything she said might come out as an accusation, not that one from her would be worse than what he already faced. "Can you tell me what happened?" she said.

"I don't know, girl," her father said. "I don't know how I got into the pantry. I remember only bits and pieces of yesterday afternoon and evening." Meilyr's brow furrowed, and then he shook his head. "I have a memory of making music during the evening meal ... unless that was the day before? But after that ... I don't remember anything that happened until the cook screamed in my ear and I saw Collen dead at my feet."

Gwen bit her lip. "You were supposed to meet me in the herbalist's hut after we sang in the hall for Lord Cadfael. I practiced by myself until well past moonrise because you never came."

Meilyr gazed down at his feet. "Could I have stopped for a quick drink in private?"

Gwen suppressed the groan that formed in her chest. Her father certainly could have done that, though she'd hoped that he'd put those days behind him. At the same time, she was pleased that even in his decrepit state, he was aware enough of the hold drink had over him to ask the question of himself before she could.

"You never saw Collen?" she said.

Meilyr's eyes shifted to the left, just like Gwalchmai's did when he lied to her, even as her father shook his head and said, "No."

Gwen glared at him. "You did see him. When?"

Meilyr scrubbed at his graying hair. He had been allowed to wash the blood from his hands before they put him in the cell. "You have no right to question me, Gwen. I didn't kill the man. That's all you need to know."

Gwen was afraid that her father still didn't seem to understand the seriousness of his situation, nor understand that if he was convicted of murder, his children would suffer too. "It's not me you have to convince," Gwen said. "It's Gruffydd, Robert, and Lord Cadfael."

"They are all good men," Meilyr said.

Gwen felt her temper rising. "Good men? If any one of them believes you murdered Collen, as it seems both Gruffydd and Robert already do, Lord Cadfael could hang you! What will happen to Gwalchmai and me, then?"

"Cadfael won't hang me. Why would he?"

"Because you killed Collen!"

Meilyr shook his head. "I don't know why you're talking about a hanging. At the most, the *galanas* I am required to pay will be more than we can afford."

Gwen shook her head, a deep unease in her bones. "We're in the south, Father, not in Gwynedd. Even if King Anarawd is in the ascendency now, the Normans have a strong hold here. We don't know if Lord Cadfael will abide by the old laws." Payment of *galanas* from the murderer to the victim's family was the traditional Welsh method of punishing a murderer. Punishment by dismemberment and death was a Norman innovation, though one that some Welsh lords were employing despite the law.

"Don't talk that way," Meilyr said.

"Don't you understand how bad this looks?" Gwen said. "Remember what happened to Gareth!"

At the mention of Gareth's name, the tension between Gwen and her father filled the room to the point that Gwen could almost see it. Her father sat still, just looking at Gwen. She stared at her feet. She'd sworn she wouldn't say Gareth's name, ever again, even if she'd thought about him every day since she was sixteen years old.

Her first love—and her only one—Gareth had been a man-at-arms in the service of Prince Cadwaladr, ruler of

Ceredigion. Gareth had wanted to marry Gwen but had been dismissed from Cadwaladr's service before he could. His single act of disobedience—the refusal to cut off the hand of a young thief—had reverberated through all their lives. Cadwaladr had been angry, impetuous, and unreasonable, and Gwen feared that in respect to her father, Cadfael might be the same.

Meilyr cleared his throat. "Just because I don't remember what passed during the evening, doesn't mean Lord Cadfael will think I killed my old friend."

"Robert certainly thinks you did, and he will testify to Lord Cadfael to that effect," Gwen said.

Meilyr rubbed at his chin. "Somebody wants it to look like I did it."

"But why?"

Meilyr snorted. "So it doesn't look like they did it, of course." Meilyr's voice was all patience, as if Gwen had the intelligence of Dai, the castle's resident imbecile who hauled the slops from the kitchen and cleaned the latrine.

"But why you?" Gwen said.

"I don't know."

"You made it so easy for the killer. You walked right into his trap."

Meilyr snorted, though whether at Gwen or in agreement with her, Gwen didn't know. She closed her eyes, trying to rein in her temper. She shouldn't have shouted at her father, but she hadn't been able to help herself. Thankfully, he hadn't felt the need to slap her down just now.

"You must speak to Gruffydd," Gwen said. "He's very certain that you killed Collen, but if you tell him about your loss of memory, it might introduce a morsel of doubt."

Meilyr leaned back against the wall. "He won't listen to me, not unless someone else comes forward to support what I have to say."

Gwen eyed him. "Father, despite your denials, are you worried that you might have killed Collen?"

Meilyr shrugged.

"Why would you think that of yourself, even if you were drunk?" Gwen said.

"He and I had a slight disagreement yesterday," Meilyr said.

So that was what he'd been hiding. "The disagreement was serious enough to make you want to kill him?" Gwen said.

Meilyr tipped his head back and forth to say *maybe.* "Not when I'm sober."

"A disagreement over what?" Gwen said. "You've always liked Collen."

"Which is why I didn't want to tell you or Gruffydd what passed between us," Meilyr said. "He and I discussed the formation of a business relationship, since I travel through Wales as much as he does."

Gwen's eyes narrowed. "This business relationship would have involved what, exactly?"

Meilyr tsked through his teeth. "He proposed that I might carry an item or two for him from one place to the next, at which point he'd collect it and pay me for my time."

Gwen didn't like the sound of that. "What kind of items?" she said, and then she bit her lip when she recognized from the impassivity in her father's face what he meant. "Collen was talking about stolen items! He wanted you to smuggle valuables out of a castle for him! As a bard, nobody would suspect you, and then he would meet you later to collect what he'd stolen."

Meilyr canted his head. "As you say."

Gwen shook her head in disbelief. "Did you agree?"

"Obviously not," Meilyr said. "I thought about it, though not for long. It simply wouldn't have been worth the risk, not with Gwalchmai's voice being what it is."

Gwen nodded. Gwalchmai's voice was going to be their entry into any hall in any cantref for many years to come. His soprano already rivaled that of the finest singers in Wales. In a few years his voice would change, true, but with his knowledge of music and poetry, instilled by her father who was himself a poet and scholar, Gwalchmai could become one of the most revered bards of his generation. That, at least, was her father's plan. He had stopped over-drinking because of that promise. He would do nothing to jeopardize it.

"What about the mead?" Gwen said.

Meilyr shook his head. "I don't know. I don't remember drinking any."

"What do you mean, you don't remember?" Gwen said, her voice rising again. "You clearly had a great deal of it."

Meilyr opened his mouth, perhaps to deny her words, but then he closed it and shifted awkwardly on his bench. "I did not mean to imbibe."

"Then why did you?"

"I don't remember."

Gwen felt like ripping out her hair and knew that she was going to ruin the most civil conversation she'd had with her father in months, even if it was about murder. "You *know* that on bad days you can't even have one sip without falling into drunkenness. And look. That's exactly what you've done."

A knock came at the door before her father could answer, and Gwen turned away in relief. Saran, the herbalist, poked her head into the room. "You asked to see me, Gwen?"

Saran was of middle-age, comfortably-figured, and as far as Gwen knew, had never married. Her coal-black hair was braided and coiled in a rope around her head. Gwen had seen it down once. It fell almost to her ankles.

Gwen ran to the door and took both of Saran's hands in hers. "Yes! Thank you for coming!" She pulled Saran into the cell and once again, the guard shut the door behind them.

"Hello, Meilyr." Saran stopped in front of the bard, who lifted his head. He'd been coherent while he'd conversed with Gwen, but his eyes were still bleary.

"Hello, Saran."

"What have you got yourself into this time?" Saran put her fingers underneath Meilyr's chin and turned his head from side to side. "You don't look well."

"I had too much to drink," Meilyr said.

Gwen was surprised that he admitted it, but he seemed comfortable in Saran's presence.

"Hmmm ... it's something else, I think," Saran said.

"What do you mean?" Gwen stepped closer.

Saran leaned in and sniffed before turning to Gwen. "Do you smell that?"

Gwen felt awkward standing so close to her father and sniffing at him, but she did as Saran asked. "Yes. I ..." Gwen thought a moment. "Edain said he smelled something sweet or nutty on Collen's breeches earlier, before they took him from the pantry."

Saran nodded. "It's not drink, Meilyr, though you certainly had plenty of that, too. Or at least your clothing did."

"Then what is it?" Meilyr said.

"It's an old recipe, from the east," Saran said. "A skilled herbalist pours it into a sponge and holds it under a patient's nostrils, to ease their pain and help them to sleep."

"What is in it?" Gwen said.

"It's an infusion of poppy, mandrake, hemlock, and ivy," Saran said.

Gwen's heart beat a little faster. "Such a concoction can't be easy to acquire."

"I wouldn't have said so," Saran said.

"But you think someone could have used it on my father?"

"It would certainly explain Meilyr's deep sleep," Saran said. "Even a drunkard should notice when a man is murdered at his feet."

"I'm not a drunkard!" Meilyr said.

Saran bent to look into Meilyr's face. "You are. I've kept my eye on you and even if you've been sober most of this winter, if you are going to live through tomorrow and help that boy of yours become everything you hope he does, you need to admit it. And drink only water."

Meilry made a disgusted noise in his throat, but then said, "You're right. I know—" He clenched his knees so hard that his knuckles turned white. "I hate water."

Saran shook her head. "Did you kill Collen?"

"No." Meilyr's voice was stronger again.

Saran muttered something that included the words "men" and "stubborn" as she looked down on Meilyr's bowed head. Then Saran spoke louder: "Elements of this crime seemed to have been well-planned, in that your father was deliberately dosed with this infusion and put into the pantry. But other aspects, like the strangling of Collen are that of impulse. Surely there are cleaner ways to kill a man."

"At the same time, it's hard to imagine a method more effective than a harp string," Gwen said.

Again, the muttering, before Saran raised her voice. "True. Though I could tell you better."

Gwen didn't dare ask about that knowledge. A skilled herbalist, by definition, was the most trusted—and the most dangerous—person in any community.

"Will you go to Gruffydd with this?" Gwen said.

Saran glanced at Gwen. "I will, but it won't be enough."

The pit of sickness in Gwen's stomach threatened to become permanent. "It won't?"

Saran straightened, patted Meilyr on the shoulder, and then took Gwen's arm. "Come with me." Saran prodded Gwen to the door, knocked on it, and when the guard opened it, hurried Gwen through it and out of the barracks. Saran halted and turned to Gwen, her eyes full of regret. "It will not be enough that I bring my suspicions to Gruffydd. There is too much evidence weighing against your father for Lord Cadfael to release him on my word."

"Wha—what do you mean?" Tears formed in Gwen's eyes.

"*Cariad*, why are you crying?"

"B—b—because my father has been accused of murder." Gwen brushed away the tears with the back of her hands.

Saran's gentleness gave way to impatience. She stood with her hands on her hips, waiting for Gwen to regain control. Gwen struggled not to cry for another dozen heartbeats and then managed a shaky smile.

"That's better," Saran said. "Now. We know that Gruffydd and Robert have already made up their minds about your father, correct?"

Gwen nodded, not daring to speak lest Saran's exasperation overflowed again.

"Has Gruffydd tried to trace your father's movements last night? Has he talked to anyone at all?"

"Not that I know," Gwen said.

Saran gave a sharp nod. "Then I guess it is up to you."

"What?" Gwen said. "How could it be up to me?"

"I've watched you for three months, now," Saran said, "moping about, pining after that Gareth of yours."

"I'm not pin—"

"You are, and it's time you stopped. He's not coming back and you need to manage your own life instead of hoping that someone else is always going to be there to take care of you. What will you do if your father is convicted of Collen's murder? How will you care for your brother? Where will you go?"

"I don't know—"

"Exactly. You don't know. But you could know. You could have a plan. And maybe while you're thinking of one, you could find out something that will help your father. You have a mind. Use it!"

Gwen's mouth opened and closed. She didn't know what to say. "I do use it—"

"When you first arrived, months ago, I offered to teach you about herbs, to give you a useful skill for when you weren't at the beck and call of your father and brother. What did I get from you?" Saran went on without waiting for Gwen's response. "Nothing! A shrug at most."

"I'm sorry. I didn't mean to be rude. I'm a bard's daughter—"

"You'll be a murderer's daughter if you're not careful," Saran said.

Gwen stood gazing at Saran with her fists to her lips and her mouth open. She dropped her hands to her sides. "I didn't think—"

"Well, start thinking!" Saran spun on her heel and marched away

All Gwen could do was stare after her.

3

"Young lady," Robert said. "Your father murdered a man. Lord Cadfael cannot let such an act go unpunished." Robert stood before Gwen, his brows furrowed and his lips turned down. He wore his gray hair close cut and he ran a hand through it as if to imply that he couldn't believe Gwen had the temerity to question him.

Gwen couldn't quite believe it either. "I know that the murderer must be punished. But my father didn't kill anyone."

Gruffydd had been standing beside the steward and now bent at the waist to bring his face down to Gwen's level so he could look into her eyes. It was better than Robert looking down his nose at her. "Meilyr killed Collen, Gwen. We found him next to the body."

"My father has no marks on him, even if he did have blood on his hands," Gwen said. "How could he have slit

Collen's throat so easily? Collen was half again my father's size."

This was true. Gwen was neither tall nor short, but her father was of less than average height, only a few inches taller than Gwen. In his middle years, his body had grown soft and he'd developed something of a paunch, which he tried to hide beneath his generously cut tunic. Collen, by comparison, was fitter. Even though he was closer in age to Meilyr than to Gwen, he didn't look it. Or hadn't.

"Men have been known to show great strength when angered," Gruffydd said. "He would have attacked Collen from behind. Upon Collen's death, the body would have fallen just as it did and your father's clothing would have remained clean."

Gwen bit her lip. She was hoping to find an additional argument that would prompt Gruffydd to admit some measure of doubt, so then she could have saved the more powerful reasoning for last. As it was … "I know that my father was found with the body, and that the harp string belongs to him. He even had blood on his hands, but Saran says that there's more to it than that."

"How so?" Lord Cadfael had been sitting at one end of the high table, observing their conversation without participating in it. Gwen had been careful not to involve him.

She didn't want to draw the wrath of either Robert or Gruffydd by going over his head to his lord. Given the direction the conversation had taken, however, it might be unavoidable.

"Because he was dosed with a potion. Did you not notice a strange smell about him?" Gwen's eyes were on Gruffydd as she spoke.

Gruffydd breathed deeply through his nose, as a man might do whose patience is sorely tried. "I did not. What of this smell?"

"It comes from a potion from the east that will put a man into a deep sleep with a few sniffs," Gwen said.

"I find that unlikely." Robert adjusted his fine, deep green tunic with a jerk. As steward for Lord Cadfael, he was a wealthy man in his own right and dressed accordingly.

Gwen gazed at Robert and then back to Gruffydd, her own patience stretched to the limit. "Let's say he was dosed with it. Where could the murderer have gotten such a rare potion?"

Gruffydd shrugged. "I respect Saran's wisdom, but with the mead your father had consumed ..."

Robert rocked back and forth on the balls on his feet. "He was very drunk."

"That is exactly my point, my lords." Gwen forced herself to moderate her tone before it rose. It was all very well and good for Saran to chastise Gwen for not actively trying to help her father, but it was quite another to get these men to listen to her. But then, she was a girl, and Robert was Cadfael's right hand man, while Gruffydd ruled the garrison. Why *should* they listen to her?

Then Cadfael surprised Gwen by saying, "It can't do any harm to search the pantry. If the girl is right and her father is innocent, then the real murderer could have dosed her father. You might find the cloth or bottle nearby."

Gwen curtseyed. "Thank you, my lord—"

Cadfael cut her off, baring his teeth. "And if you don't find it, we can dismiss this as the nonsense it is."

"But, my lord—" Robert said.

"She's a pretty girl who loves her father." Lord Cadfael pushed to his feet. "Humor her, Gruffydd. At least look for a sign that what she says might be true."

"Thank you, my lord," Gwen said, again. "Really, my father didn't kill this man. Collen was his friend. He had no reason to kill him."

Robert smirked. "Didn't he, my dear? It looks to me as if he was caught red-handed ... so to speak."

Cadfael waved a hand. "Don't try to complicate what is really very simple." He left the room.

Gwen bent her head to gaze at her toes, hating that they were treating her like a little girl but unable to do anything about it. "My father didn't kill Collen."

"Then who did?" Robert said. "If you're so sure, you find him." Robert turned on one heel to follow Cadfael.

Gwen's head came up. *What?* Although Saran had said as much—perhaps more as a goad than because it was a reasonable thing to do—the very fact that Robert would suggest the same thing left Gwen gasping. Wasn't this Gruffydd's job? Did none of these men care that if Meilyr hadn't killed Collen, a murderer remained loose in the castle?

Whenever he saw her, Prince Hywel of Gwynedd, Gwen's friend since childhood, loved to question Gwen about the details and gossip of life outside of Gwynedd. They'd grown up together at Aberffraw, King Owain's seat on Anglesey in the northwest of Wales. Hywel, as the second, bastard son of the King, found his place in the order of things at the royal court precarious and collected information as a way to stay one step ahead of anyone who might challenge him or his father.

The last time she'd seen Hywel, he'd questioned her particularly closely. Since then, she'd begun to pay attention to the less savory aspects of court life, which were more common than she would have liked to admit. She'd never thought her discoveries would go beyond unfaithful wives or straying husbands, into the world of thievery and smuggling—such as Collen had asked of her father—or murder.

"I suppose I will have to see to this," Gruffydd said to no one in particular, since both of his superiors had already left the room.

Gwen curtseyed to Gruffydd, desperate to smooth his ruffled feathers. He merely nodded that she should follow him, so she trailed behind him, out of the hall and to the kitchen, behind which lay the entrance to the pantry. They entered the kitchen through a wide doorway that was kept open to the winter air at all times. Even so, the kitchen was warm and smoky—hot even—with its two fireplaces going at once, one for baking and another for the stew that simmered in its pot. The fires burned the day long and into the night, necessary for feeding all the residents of the castle.

The interior of Carreg Cennen Castle was relatively simple, with the usual complement of keep, stable, barracks, blacksmith works, kitchen, and craft huts. To protect the great hall from fire, the kitchen was separated from the main buildings by a covered pathway. Gwen's only complaint was that her family had very little privacy here, which was why she and Gwalchmai had resorted to the herbalist's hut to rehearse their music. When her father hadn't appeared to practice with her the previous evening as he'd promised, she'd had to go over the particularly difficult piece they were singing tomorrow by herself.

When she'd gone as far with the song as she could, she'd left the hut to search for him, but nobody had seen him. The performance would be for the birth day feast of Lord Cadfael's eldest son, who was turning fourteen, and what puzzled her particularly about her father's absence was that it was he who had asked her to meet him, intent on getting the song exactly right. A boy became a man only once in a lifetime, and for Cadoc, that would be tomorrow.

Because of the upcoming celebration, the kitchens were busier than usual, in that they were not only preparing meals to feed the several dozen residents of the castle, but to fill the stomachs of guests who had come from miles around. Among these guests were farmers and merchants who tithed to Cadfael, plus peasants, laborers, and shepherds, none of whom wanted to miss the opportunity for several satisfying meals.

Gwen felt the eyes of every person in the kitchen on her. The people here had always been friendly to Gwen, but another shiver of dread trailed down her spine at their distrustful looks. Gruffydd took her elbow and she walked with him to the rear door and then along the path that led to the underground pantry. Her knees trembled as she descended the ladder behind Gruffydd.

Gwen had hoped never to enter here again, and was relieved to see that the body had been removed to the chapel in preparation for burial, though that might not be possible until the winter cold let up and the ground softened. From the look of the floor, someone had attempted to scrub the stones clean of Collen's blood, with minimal success. The blood itself was gone. The stain remained.

"What are we looking for?" Gruffydd said. "A vial?"

"And a cloth or sponge, maybe?" Gwen said. "According to Saran, they would smell sweet and nutty."

Gwen felt she had made significant progress just in getting Gruffydd to come search with her. She began peering behind discarded barrels and patting her hand into the crevices in the stones and under the empty shelves. Gruffydd pulled aside the curtain that blocked the entrance to the long tunnel at the far end of the room that led deeper into the mountain. He walked down the passage until Gwen lost sight of him and could see only the bob and weave of his lantern.

After he'd returned and they'd covered both sides of the room, they met again in the center. Gruffydd stood glaring down at the blood stain on the floor. Gwen waited.

"No vial," he said.

"Not that I can find. But my father was dosed." Gwen's hands fisted. He *was*.

Gruffydd grunted. "We'll see." He turned away, but Gwen clutched at his sleeve.

"Have you questioned the kitchen staff? Has anyone come forward to say they saw my father?"

"No."

Despite what Saran had suggested, Gruffydd's accompanying shrug caught Gwen off guard. "You haven't talked to anyone about what happened last night, have you?" she said.

"We know who murdered Collen."

"Please ... please. Don't make any judgments just yet," Gwen said.

Gruffydd fingered his chin and gazed at Gwen. Then, he took in a deep breath and let it out. "I will make some inquiries."

Gwen eased out a sigh. "Thank you. Thank you so much."

Gruffydd looked down at her. "You have a little time. Lord Cadfael has said that he will not sully his son's birth day tomorrow with a hanging."

"A hanging?" Gwen had used the word with her father, more to shock him into making sense than because she'd really thought Cadfael would hang him. To hear the word come from Gruffydd's mouth turned her stomach to stone. "What about payment of *galanas*?"

"In certain instances, payment isn't enough. You know that. It never has been. King Anarawd said as much at the Christmas feast when he called all his barons to him. He is specifically concerned about treason, but he has hung men for murder in the past."

"How can that be?" Gwen said. "The law—"

"The law of Wales is clear," Gruffydd said, "but the Normans encroach on us at every turn. If a lord doesn't maintain a tight control on his people—and his lands—he might lose them."

Gwen ground her teeth. Norman law stated that a man must hang for the murder of another man, but the laws of Hywel Dda said that each individual person—each man, woman and child—had a value. In Wales, a man paid *galanas*—compensation—to the family of the one he'd killed.

"We are Welsh, not Norman!" Gwen said.

"Lord Cadfael feels that he must make an example of Meilyr, lest others equally lose their way." Gruffydd touched one finger to Gwen's shoulder and then dropped his hand. "We live in difficult times, Gwen. The old ways are no longer sufficient."

"How can you say that?"

"You have until the day after tomorrow. Meilyr will stand before Cadfael then and receive his sentence."

As Gruffydd departed, Gwen sagged to her knees on the cold stone of the floor. She had two days.

4

Gwen understood that it was often difficult for men to admit they were wrong, especially to a woman, so she didn't follow Gruffydd when he left the pantry or press him further. She had never thought him an ignorant man, nor one who would willfully hang a man out of convenience. But it seemed he intended to do so this time. At least Cadfael had allowed him to search for evidence of a different killer.

Gwen didn't really know how to proceed, but she decided that her first task was to question those who knew Collen, under the principle that his death was not a random act of a complete stranger. Gwen didn't have any idea how she would know when she learned something that would help her, but she didn't know where else to start. She had to hope that she would recognize a clue when she saw it.

Collen had traveled Wales with a small cart, which he'd parked in a lean-to attached to the stable. Either he or his servant, Ifan, who traveled with him, always guarded it. Ifan had come to Collen at the age of eight. He was eighteen now, and after ten years of working with Collen, was more like a son than a servant. His presence allowed Collen to work his deals without leaving his possessions unprotected. Ifan always slept in, on, or near the cart. In fact, when Gwen thought about it, she realized that the only time she'd seen him leave it was to use the latrine.

As she expected, this morning he sat where he always did: on a short stool, whittling a piece of wood with a small knife. His hands were encased in thick gloves, as were those of every other man in the castle on this winter day.

Gwen came to a halt in front of him. Now that she was here, her tongue stuck to the roof of her mouth. She managed to speak around it. "I'm sorry for your loss."

Ifan looked up at her, ducked his head once, and went back to his whittling, whistling tunelessly through his teeth. Even with only the brief glance, Gwen couldn't miss the dirty tracks of tears on his cheeks. Not long ago, he'd been weeping.

Gwen pursed her lips, feeling intensely uncomfortable, but she felt she must continue what she'd started. "Where were you last night?" Gwen tried to keep the question casual, hoping to deceive Ifan into thinking that she was merely curious, instead of intensely interested.

Ifan shrugged. "Right here. It's where I always am."

"Always?" Gwen said.

Ifan stopped his whittling to look up at her again. He barked a laugh. "Are you accusing me of having something to do with Collen's death?"

"We don't know when Collen died exactly," Gwen said. "Maybe you were the one to kill him. Maybe you've grown tired of being his servant."

"I was like a son to him," Ifan said. "Why would I wish for his death?"

"The cart, for one thing," Gwen said, "and everything in it. With Collen's death, you can strike out on your own."

Ifan shook his head. "No." He spat on the ground. "Lord Cadfael told me just now that everything Collen owned belongs to either Collen's partner or his widow. I get nothing. I don't even own the clothes on my back, though I'll go straight to hell before I let anyone take them from me." The tears were gone and Ifan's face had gone red as his temper had risen.

Gwen decided it was time to divert the conversation. "I didn't know Collen had a partner or a widow. He never spoke of them."

"He kept his business to himself," Ifan said.

"Do you know where either the partner or the widow live?" Gwen said. "Someone has to tell them that Collen is dead."

"They already know," Ifan said. "The widow, Eva, arrived at mid-day yesterday. The partner, Denis, met us on the road and entered Carreg Cennen when we did, three days ago."

Gwen and her family had spent the winter at Carreg Cennen Castle, so Gwen was surprised that she'd missed out on any talk or gossip about Collen. She'd not spoken to the man more than once or twice in passing since he arrived, but she was observant enough to note that he hadn't sat with anyone in particular at the meal last night.

Then again, as Ifan had pointed out, Collen kept his business to himself, except when he wanted something—like her father to smuggle goods for him. She *believed* her father when he'd told her that he'd turned Collen down, and that he hadn't been angry. Could he have lied to her, even about something as important as this?

And then she admonished herself for her naïveté, because of course he could. Her father had been stern and distant all through her growing up and at times she'd hated him for it. He'd always had his mind directed towards his own well-being, and that of Gwalchmai. Ever since Gwalchmai's birth, and her mother's death in birthing him, Meilyr's only use for Gwen was as a child-minder. But he loved Gwalchmai and she believed him when he said that he would do nothing to jeopardize his future.

"May I look through Collen's things?" Gwen said. "It might help us discover who murdered him."

"Everyone knows who murdered him," Ifan said. "Your father."

"My father didn't have anything to do with this," Gwen said. "He couldn't have." She'd lost track of the number of times she'd said those words. And yet, in the face of everyone else's staunch certainty, a wavering voice had begun in her head, wondering if it was others she was trying to convince—or herself.

"I heard he was found with the body. *And* I heard what he said to Collen last night." Ifan sneered. "Wait until I tell Gruffydd of it. It will be the final nail in his coffin."

Gwen licked her lips. Her father hadn't said anything about an open fight, and certainly not one that had been loud enough for Ifan to hear. But if Ifan knew of it, who else might speak of it to Gruffydd? "What did you hear? When? Please tell me."

"It was last night." Ifan stuck out his chin. "Collen and Meilyr were at each other's throats in the stable." He pointed with his knife towards the planks to his left that formed the side wall of the stable. "They didn't shout, but their words were fierce. They wouldn't have known I could hear them. People always think that a wall keeps sound in when it doesn't."

"I already know what they discussed," Gwen said. "My father told me. Collen wanted my father to smuggle a stolen item out of Carreg Cennen."

Ifan snorted his disbelief. "That's what he told you, did he? If that were true, why did Meilyr call Collen a *cheating bastard*?"

Gwen eyed Ifan. "He didn't. You made that up."

"I speak the truth," Ifan said. "Collen had promised your father a gift for helping him arrange a trading partnership with Lord Cadfael."

"And Collen refused to give it?" Gwen said. "Why would he do that?"

Ifan shrugged. "Because he never gave away anything he didn't have to. Your father threatened to kill him."

Gwen stared at him. This was getting worse by the hour. She hadn't thought that was possible. "I know my father didn't kill Collen." Gwen had no intention of letting

Ifan know he was getting to her. "And you say you didn't, but if I prove my father's innocence, on whom will suspicion fall next? Who would be Gruffydd's easiest target?"

"Not me," Ifan said. "I had nothing to gain."

"Prove it," Gwen said. "Let me search the cart."

To Gwen's surprise, Ifan shrugged. "Nothing in there belongs to me anyway." He pushed up from his stool, his booted feet scuffling in the loose hay beneath his feet. He unlatched the flap that protected Collen's goods and raised it. Then he stepped aside, making room for Gwen.

Gwen stepped up and began picking through the shelves and drawers that Collen had cleverly built into his mobile market stall. But while Gwen saw plenty of items she might want for herself, she didn't see a discarded vial. It had been silly to think she would. Ifan wasn't the smartest boy in the castle, but if he was the murderer, surely he would have known better than to keep evidence of his guilt. And as he said, what had he to gain from Collen's death?

Gwen rubbed her forehead with her fingers, feeling a headache coming on. She closed her eyes, trying to focus on what she should do next.

"You might talk to Collen's partner," Ifan said. "And to the widow, Eva."

"I will do that. I'm sorry to bother you at a time like this."

Ifan lifted one shoulder in acknowledgement of the apology. Gwen turned away, though not without casting a last glance at the servant. He had lowered himself onto his stool again, this time with his back to the courtyard—and to her. Gwen left him to himself, but instead of returning to the hall to look for Eva or Denis, she ducked under the eaves of the stable.

As she stood in the doorway, allowing her eyes to adjust to the lack of light, a vision of another day and a different stable rose before her eyes. That time, she hadn't been alone. Gareth had been with her.

Gareth.

She'd spent her days watching for him, waiting for him to return from patrol, or bringing him food from the kitchen. On one of the days he'd been let off from his duties, she'd searched him out. He had been currying his horse in the stable. A thong at the base of his neck secured his dark hair, though bits of straw had still managed to stick in it. She'd plucked one out, and as he'd looked at her, she'd known that he was the best thing ever to happen to her. It had all felt so *right*.

She'd cried in his arms when he'd told her he was leaving. She'd railed at him at the time, but he'd explained firmly that he had to live with himself, no matter where he lived. He couldn't obey Prince Cadwaladr's orders, any more than he could stop loving her. Sometimes a man had to stand up for what was right, lest he lose his immortal soul.

But his loss of station meant that he couldn't provide for her and thus, Meilyr had refused to give Gwen to him. Although Gwen had looked for Gareth in every place they'd stopped since, she'd never seen him again. As Gwen allowed her eyes to adjust to the shadows in the stable, she told herself that Saran was right. He was gone. Gwen had to admit that it was forever. He could even be dead.

Yet even so, he remained with her and the same feeling of certainty—of *rightness*—that she'd felt when she stood with Gareth in that stable years ago came over her again now. She had been looking at this task all wrong. It wasn't her job to prove her father innocent. It was to find the truth, no matter where that led her. All her life, she'd leaned on others—on her mother, on Gareth, on her father, even as she resented her dependency—and now there was nobody left to lean on but herself.

Gwen choked under her breath. How was she to find her own way? Discovering the identity of Collen's murderer paled in comparison to standing on her own two feet.

Even so, the only way to reach tomorrow was through today. Gwen turned towards the wall of the stable where Ifan had said Collen and her father had argued. Gwen lifted the lantern that hung by the stable door and brought it with her, peering at the floor near the wall.

Her bad luck held and there was nothing to see there but dirty straw and a packed earthen floor. She'd hoped to find something that would help her piece together the night's events. It wasn't that she didn't believe her father, or Ifan, necessarily, but that one of the things Gareth had impressed upon her was that she shouldn't take anyone's word (but his) without confirming it for herself.

Sadly, such a stance eroded trust, but it was good advice when one's father was accused of murder.

"What are you doing?"

Gwen swung around at the voice, to see one of the stable boys, Wyn, leaning on his hay fork in the closest stall. He was friends with Edain and they were of an age, though where Edain was tall and lanky, Wyn hadn't come into his growth yet. She knew enough of fourteen year old boys to know that it irked him to be shorter than all his friends, but from the size of his feet, that growth would come soon. Last week, when he had been looking morose, she'd even told him so.

"Just looking," Gwen said.

Wyn peered past her. "For what?" His voice didn't hold suspicion, just curiosity.

"Did you overhear an argument between my father and Collen the trader yesterday?" Gwen said.

Wyn's forehead furrowed. "No."

Gwen's shoulders fell. If anyone had heard them, it would have been Wyn.

Then the Wyn's eyes brightened. "But I did see Meilyr with a woman later in the evening."

Gwen's chin came up. "You saw my father with a woman? What woman?"

Wyn shrugged. "I didn't see her face. I didn't see much of any of her. She wore a cloak with the hood pulled up."

"Was she short, tall, have dark hair—what?" Gwen's heart raced. Perhaps she hadn't lost her mind. Perhaps there really was more to this than Robert and Gruffydd thought.

"I don't know. She was shorter than he, anyway, with a laugh that carried. I saw them in here after the evening meal, after the singing had finished in the hall. They left the stable for the kitchen garden arm in arm."

"Did they really?" Gwen said. That didn't sound much like her father. As far as she knew, and she'd been paying attention, he hadn't spent the evening with a woman more than a few times in the last ten years, and not at all at Carreg Cennen. "How do you know that the man she was with was my father?"

"I would recognize his voice anywhere," the boy said.

Gwen had to grant that this was true. Her father's rich baritone had filled many a hall over the years. He had even been the court bard for the King of Gwynedd until the old king's death. Their troubles had started after that, when the king's son, Owain Gwynedd, hadn't immediately confirmed Meilyr in his position. Her father had been offended and the two men had fallen out over it.

Or rather, her father had been short of temper, King Owain had been stubborn, and Meilyr had taken Gwen and Gwalchmai away from Aberffraw, never to return. That was years ago and they hadn't re-entered Gwynedd since.

"So you wouldn't know this woman again if you saw her?" Gwen said.

Wyn shook his head. "I think I would recognize anyone who lived here. She has to be one of the visitors to the castle."

"The castle is full of visitors today," Gwen said. "You really didn't see anything more?"

"I didn't follow them, if that's what you're asking." Wyn laughed. "As if I would be stupid enough to eavesdrop on your father. He would have had my head."

"True." Gwen patted Wyn on the shoulder. "Thank you for your help."

"You're welcome." Wyn took the lantern and hung it back on its hook. But then he stopped Gwen before she could leave the stable. "Don't take this the wrong way, but none of us here are sorry that your father killed Collen. It makes him a bit of a hero, actually."

"It does?" Gwen froze in the doorway and turned back to Wyn. "How is that?"

"Collen whipped his horse over much," Wyn said. To a stable lad, that was a crime worthy of severe punishment. "I'm surprised Ifan didn't mention it."

"Why would he?" Gwen said.

"Because Collen whipped him too." Wyn began forking hay into a pile.

Gwen watched him work for another few heartbeats. Gareth had commented once that you never really knew some people until they were dead. It looked like that might be true for Collen.

5

"What's going to happen to us?" Gwalchmai said.

With the waning of the day, Gwen had gone in search of Gwalchmai. She found him sitting where she'd last seen him earlier that morning: in a miserable heap on a stool in a corner of the kitchen. Not even his usual cheerful personality could overcome their father's imprisonment.

"Nothing bad. We are going to survive this," Gwen said, "no matter what happens to Father."

"How do you know?" Gwalchmai said.

"Because I'm going to see to it," Gwen said.

"How am I supposed to sing tonight with Father locked away like this?" The question came out a wail.

Gwen stared at him. "Who said you were supposed to sing tonight?" She checked the open kitchen door. The sun had been gone for some time now. The kitchen was full of men and women, running in and out of the door with serving platters for the diners in the hall.

"Lord Cadfael."

"And you agreed?"

Gwalchmai's eyebrows came together. "Of course, I did. I sing every night. But tonight, because so many guests came early for the celebration, Lord Cadfael asked me to honor them. He requested Taliesin's *Battle of the Trees* especially."

Gwen clasped her hands and put them to her lips, studying her brother over them. At times like this one, he seemed very far from a little boy. That song was one of the more challenging in his repertoire. It was not only very long, but had an intricate melody. Gwalchmai knew it by heart, however.

"I guess you should sing, then, since he asked. We have to earn our keep. Perhaps it will encourage Cadfael to look upon our family in a friendlier way."

"Surely he doesn't blame us for what Father has done." Gwalchmai straightened on his stool, gathering himself together, the worry of a moment ago forgotten. "Besides, if you're right that Father is innocent, all the more reason for us to continue as if nothing is wrong."

"What do you need from me?" Gwen said. "Have you eaten?"

Gwalchmai nodded, far more composed at the thought of performing before a hundred people than many—if not most—adults might be. "I'm ready."

Gwen walked with Gwalchmai into the hall through a rear door. No one looked up at their entrance. The diners were engrossed in their meal. Gwen hadn't felt like eating, but now her stomach growled at her. The hall wasn't quite as full as it would be tomorrow for Cadoc's birthday, but the tables had few empty seats. Tomorrow the people would line the walls and spill into the courtyard too.

With a nod, Gwen urged Gwalchmai ahead of her. He made his way to the dais, pausing in front of it long enough to speak briefly with Lord Cadfael, who held up a hand to him and nodded. The respect Cadfael showed Gwalchmai warmed Gwen's heart. Her brother *was* special. They all knew it. And yet, somehow, Gwalchmai was still the same sweet little brother he'd always been.

The thought of how he might be hurt by the events of today had Gwen's fists clenching. No matter what happened, she would do her best to protect him as she always had.

Gwen had expressed confidence to Gwalchmai that their father would survive this accusation—what else could she do in the face of Gwalchmai's fear?—but inside, she was worried. None of the men—Lord Cadfael, Robert, or Gruffydd—seemed at all concerned that they might have locked up the wrong man. How could Cadfael hang her father so easily?

But then again, Meilyr had never been one for making friends. Far too often, he allowed his feelings to rise to the surface for all to see, even when he wasn't drinking too much. His foul moods could affect everyone with whom he came into contact, and they possessed him more often than not, as if he walked under a dark cloud nobody else could see. He courted lords as part of his livelihood, but not very many *liked* him.

Gwen gritted her teeth, feeling rueful. And what could she say to that? She didn't like her father either.

Yet, if nothing else, she had to find the strength to do her duty as a daughter and discover the truth, for his sake and hers. Saran was right to tell her that she had to help him if she could, especially when he couldn't help himself. If in the process she discovered something that would cast further suspicion on her father, well ... she would cross that bridge when she came to it.

As Gwalchmai strummed the first notes on his lyre, Gwen settled herself onto a bench near him. Her brother would play for a while as background to the meal, and then at Cadfael's signal, he would begin to sing.

Sometimes Gwen accompanied him, but she was grateful that tonight, at least, very little would be expected of her. It was tomorrow's celebration that mattered. She eyed Cadfael, wondering if he would allow Meilyr out of his cell to sing with them, as a one last request. She felt certain that her father would want it.

As the meal progressed, Gwen watched the diners with one eye and Gwalchmai with the other. He played with a focus that Gwen could never replicate, no matter how much she practiced. She had a nice voice and a sense of rhythm, but Gwalchmai *felt* the music. It was part of what was going to make him great.

Gwen rose from her bench to get a (very) watered-down cup of mead for Gwalchmai to drink before he sang *The Battle of the Trees*, for there was no stopping once he started. But as she was crossing the hall to return to her bench, Gruffydd stood up suddenly right in front of her and she nearly spilled the cup.

"Watch it." He caught her wrist, and then visibly softened. "Sorry, Gwen. How are you doing?"

Kindness from this quarter had Gwen blinking back unexpected tears. "I am well, my lord. Worried about my father, though."

Gruffydd put a hand on Gwen's shoulder. "You do know that you and your brother will be taken care of, don't you, no matter what happens to Meilyr?"

"Wh-what do you mean?"

Gruffydd was looking at her very sincerely. "Lord Cadfael does not blame you for your father's mistake. He will find you a good husband, and Gwalchmai will have a permanent place at Carreg Cennen."

Gwen swallowed hard. "Th-thank you."

"May I assist you in any way, now?"

Gruffydd's eyes held something that Gwen knew how to interpret, even if she couldn't quite believe it. She was a bard's daughter, with a dowry far smaller than a man of Gruffydd's station would require, and few possessions beyond her clothes. Even so, his manner was one of a suitor. Gwen hadn't ever felt an interest in him before, but she arranged her features so as not to appear immediately averse to Gruffydd's attentions. At the very least, she needed him on her side.

"Actually, you can," she said. "Did you know that Collen leaves behind a widow and a partner?"

Gruffydd rubbed his chin. "I know of both. It was Denis who came to me this morning and reported that Collen was missing."

"And the wife?" Gwen said.

"They were estranged, I understand. Lord Cadfael himself told her that Collen was dead."

"Did Lord Cadfael promise to shelter her too?"

Gruffydd smirked. "It seems that Denis and she have come to an agreement already. She told Lord Cadfael that he need not trouble himself with her affairs."

"That was quick," Gwen said.

"You can see them there." Gruffydd tipped his head towards two people huddled together at the end of one of the long tables.

Gwen cast a glance towards the couple. Denis was tall and slim, with pale, unlined skin and carefully brushed hair. His blonde head contrasted well with Eva's dark locks. The pair weren't quite holding hands, but their fingers were inches apart in the middle of the table. Eva's hands were soft and white while Denis' were encased in fine leather gloves.

"Collen's body isn't even buried!" Gwen said.

"It might not be buried for some time, given the cold." Gruffydd was still looking at Gwen with gentle eyes.

"As a murderer, there also may be some question as to the location and timing of your father's burial."

Gwen shivered. "Don't say that! Please don't say that! I still have one more day to discover who killed Collen. It wasn't my father. You have to believe me!"

"Gwen—" Gruffydd had been holding Gwen's wrist all this time. He held it another moment and she let him, before she nodded to him and eased away. He let her go and she headed back to her bench.

"What was that about?" Gwalchmai said as Gwen handed him the cup.

"Everyone assumes that Father murdered Collen," Gwen said.

"I don't mean that," Gwalchmai said. "I meant with Sir Gruffydd."

Gwen stopped with her own cup halfway to her lips. "Nothing, Gwalchmai. It was nothing."

"It didn't look like nothing," Gwalchmai said.

"Just—" Gwen took a deep breath and let it out. Gwalchmai was at times far too perceptive and interested in the activities of his elders. "Just leave it."

Gwalchmai drank his mead and then set down his cup. "They don't even care about Father, do they?"

"No," Gwen said. "Nor that it makes no sense for him to have murdered Collen. Why would he have done such a thing? It gains him nothing but a death sentence."

"Who does gain by his death, Gwen?" Gwalchmai said.

Gwen's eyes narrowed as she surveyed the hall. "Two people, at least: Collen's widow, Eva, and his partner, Denis." She looked at her brother. "It turns out that they have already joined forces."

"You should talk to them." Gwalchmai elbowed her in the ribs. "I'll play one more song before *The Battle of the Trees*, something sweet to soften them up."

Gwen had to smile at that. She had very carefully left Gwalchmai out of her efforts to find the truth, but singing was harmless. Gwen rose as Gwalchmai started a ballad, and made her way along the wall to the rear of the hall, towards Eva and Denis.

As she approached, Denis looked up and Eva turned. Gwen gave an involuntary gasp. There was no other way to say it: Eva was beautiful. Her black hair, which from across the hall had looked nothing out of the ordinary, was luxurious and thick, wound around her head and held by a coif, with tendrils hanging by each ear. She had the bluest eyes Gwen had ever seen, and a pale, almost translucent skin.

As Gwen hesitated in front of her, Eva smiled. "Did you want to speak to us?"

Gwen found her throat working. She should introduce herself, but how? *Hello, my name is Gwen and my father is accused of murdering your husband?*

"I—I'm Gwen," she said.

Eva smiled. "I know." She put out a hand to Gwen. "I don't blame you for what your father has done."

Gwen knew all the color had drained from her face. "Th—thank you, but I don't believe my father would have killed Collen. He was his friend."

Eva canted her head and her eyes flicked to Denis, who stood. "I don't think this is a good time to talk." He took Gwen's arm and before she knew it, he had glided her away from Eva and towards the front door of the hall. She allowed him to urge her through the doorway and down the steps to the courtyard.

Then he pulled her off the steps and to one side before turning on her. "What do you think you're doing? Can't you see that Eva is grieving?"

"I am sorry I bothered her," Gwen said, trying not to let him intimidate her. In truth, she did feel bad that Eva had lost her husband, even if they were estranged. "But my father didn't kill Collen."

"Of course, he did," Denis said. "They had a falling out yesterday. I heard all about it."

"From whom did you hear it? Ifan?"

"From Ifan?" Denis' face contracted as he dismissed the servant. "Of course not. I heard it from Collen himself."

"Why did Collen say he and my father fought?" Gwen said.

A wary expression crossed Denis' face. "Collen asked Meilyr if he would introduce him to Prince Cadwaladr of Ceredigion. Your father refused."

Gwen swallowed down her disbelieving laughter. Could this conversation be any more strange?

In the face of her silence, Denis gazed towards Collen's cart. Gwen could just make out Ifan's shape in the darkness. As she studied Denis' profile, Gwen realized that there was something about Denis that didn't sit right with her. His demeanor, his diction, and the way he dressed, spoke to her of a man whose station was far above the one he was actually living. He presented himself more like a nobleman than a merchant.

"What did Ifan tell you?" Denis said.

Gwen hesitated, unsure if it was her place to say, but then decided that if Ifan was going to tell Gruffydd anyway, Denis would know soon enough. "He said that my father helped Collen with Lord Cadfael, and then Collen refused to acknowledge the favor."

Denis looked away, his jaw working. "That's not what Collen said to me."

"I've heard three different stories so far about the conversation between my father and Collen," Gwen said. "Many lies have been told of late."

Denis jerked his eyes back to Gwen's face. "What's that supposed to mean?"

"If my father didn't kill Collen," Gwen said, "someone else did and arranged things so the blame would fall on him. Who could have done that? And why?"

Denis snorted. "Meilyr was found beside the body with a harp string at his feet and blood on his hands. He is the murderer. You're wasting your time. He should pay Eva the *galanas* he owes her and let it go."

"If my father is found guilty, there won't be any *galanas*," Gwen said.

Denis had been looking around the courtyard, not really listening, but Gwen's words brought his attention back to her. "What did you say?"

"Sir Gruffydd told me that Lord Cadfael plans to hang my father," Gwen said.

Denis moved closer, his face only a hand's span from hers. "He wouldn't!"

"Apparently, he would," Gwen said. "In that event, Eva would receive no payment."

Denis' throat worked, but he didn't answer. Gwen smiled inwardly. Eva was beautiful, but Gwen's brief encounter with Denis told her that he admired money more than beauty. And if Eva didn't receive the *galanas*, she might not be worth his time.

"There has to be someone else with motive," Gwen said. "Please think! You were Collen's partner. Who might want him dead?" *Besides you, yourself*, which Gwen didn't say.

Denis breathed in deeply. "Robert. Robert might have a motive."

Gwen took an involuntary step back. "Robert? Why him?"

Denis looked towards the door to the hall, lit by torches on either side. "Because Collen entrusted him with three gold coins to hold for him."

"Three coins ..." Gwen breathed the words. "Where did Collen get three coins?"

Denis turned back to her, his lips a thin line. "Never mind that. Needless to say, now that Collen is dead, those coins belong to Eva, or at the very least, to me. But Robert claims to know nothing about them."

Three gold coins. A man could buy a lifetime of ease for that, or land, or whatever his heart desired. Gwen wrapped her arms around her waist, trying to offset the cold, and held on, thinking hard. Robert was in a perfect position to implicate her father, since he was a man Lord Cadfael trusted. Could it be that simple? Could Robert have killed Collen and manipulated her father so that he would take the blame?

Gwen shook her head. There was still too much she didn't know—and she was running out of time to find the answers.

6

"Pssst! Gwen!"

Gwen sat up abruptly at the sound of Edain's voice and bumped her head on the low shelf below which she'd been sleeping. The floor of Saran's hut wasn't the most comfortable place to spend the night, but it had the advantage, as before when she'd wanted to practice her music, of being private. She'd retreated here once she realized that her pallet in the upstairs room in which all the women at Carreg Cennen slept had a clear perimeter around it. Nobody wanted to sleep next to a murderer's daughter.

"Where are you?" Gwen peered into the darkness of the hut. With no moon or stars showing, she couldn't see her hand in front of her face. The fire in the brazier had burned out and Gwen shivered, pulling her cloak and then her blanket around her shoulders.

"Here!" Feet thumped on the floor and then Edain struck flint to light the candle he held. Gwen shielded her eyes from the sudden light, and then lowered her hand as her eyes adjusted to it. The glow illumined his face and the little corner in which Gwen lay.

"What is the hour?"

"Very late," Edain said.

"Why have you come?" Gwen said.

"I haven't found my bed yet because I've been thinking about your father," Edain said.

The intensity in Edain's face had Gwen fully awake. "Really? Why?"

"I've been asking around about him."

"*Asking around?*" Gwen's heart beat a little faster. "That's very nice of you but I don't want you to get into trouble on his account. Or mine."

Edain shrugged that off. "What are friends for?"

Not sure how worried she should be, Gwen twisted on her pallet so that her back rested against the wall. "Tell me."

"I spoke with Wyn in the stable and he said you talked to him."

"I did. Did he remember something else?"

"No," Edain said, "but his girl did."

"Wyn has a girl?" Gwen genuinely laughed for the first time since she'd seen her father beside Collen's body.

Edain nodded. "It's Nest, the kitchen girl. She and Wyn had ... uh ... found a quiet place in the corner of the stable to ... uh ... *talk* in private. Wyn was asleep when Nest heard people passing by, near the rear door, the one closest to the entrance to the pantry. One of the voices belonged to your father, although when he spoke, his words were slurred. The other she didn't know. At least not right away."

Gwen stared at Edain, breathless. "But she does now?"

"Nest crept to the doorway and saw the couple before they disappeared. We had a bright moon last night, if you recall. The woman was giggling and your father had his arm around her waist." Edain paused.

Gwen stared at him. "So ... who was it?"

"The moon shone full on her face. She followed your father down the ladder, but came hurrying back almost immediately. Your father didn't follow her and Nest retreated to where Wyn slept, not wanting to pry and assuming they'd had a lover's quarrel. Other than the rarity of seeing your father with a woman, she thought nothing particularly of it. She went to sleep."

Gwen's teeth ground together at Edain's insouciant grin. He was drawing this out on purpose. "Who—was—the—woman?"

"Eva, Collen's wife."

Gwen sucked a breath in so hard she started coughing. Edain leaned forward and clapped her on the back. With a hand to her chest, Gwen regained control, breathing deeply. "I hadn't expected that. She's so beautiful, and—and sweet!"

"Not so sweet, apparently, that she didn't meet with your father on the very night her husband was killed."

"In the very place her husband was killed." Gwen twirled the end of her braid around one finger. *Had Eva really dosed Meilyr with a potion and left him in the pantry?*

"If Collen was already dead, she would have seen him on the floor there," Edain said. "That would be why she came back."

"Except that she didn't raise the alarm," Gwen said. "And just left my father there by himself."

"Could she have killed Collen?" Edain said. "The rock hides sounds well. The three of them could have argued ..." His voice trailed off as he reconsidered his theory.

"What about the harp string?" Gwen said. "It's not as if my father carries one on his person. And as Nest pointed out, my father was drunk."

"Perhaps Eva brought the string to the pantry. Perhaps she intended to kill Collen all along?" Edain said. "Alternatively, if Collen was already dead when Eva and Meilyr arrived in the pantry, Eva has to be involved, else why *not* raise the alarm."

"So she could blame the murder on my father?" Gwen bit her lip. It was one thing for her to pursue this line of inquiry, but Edain was a servant. He could find himself in serious danger—or lose his position—if he helped her any more. She put a hand on his arm and squeezed once. "These are interesting thoughts, Edain. Thank you so much for coming to me."

Edain's face colored. "You're welcome. I was sure that I could help."

"It would probably be better if you didn't mention our conversation or what Nest saw to anyone else, not until we know more," Gwen said. "A murderer is still loose in the castle and I don't want anyone else to get hurt."

"If you say so, Gwen." Edain ducked his head.

"And you might say the same to Nest. She and Wyn are the only ones I've found so far who saw my father last evening."

Edain's brow furrowed. "You're worried for them? You think they could be in danger?"

"We don't know why Collen was killed," Gwen said. "My father is in a cell, which might make people feel safe, but if my father didn't do it, then somebody else did. I'd like to know who that is before you, Nest, or Wyn expose yourselves by coming forward as witnesses on my father's behalf."

Edain studied Gwen for a moment without speaking. Then he nodded and rose to his feet. "We'll be careful." He touched Gwen's shoulder and disappeared through the far doorway, leaving Gwen again in darkness.

In retrospect, Gwen was surprised that only Nest and Wyn had seen her father and Eva together, and only Nest saw Eva closely enough to recognize her. Carreg Cennen was crowded with people, and yet, perhaps that made it all the easier to carry out a plan to murder Collen and implicate her father. With so many strangers, the usual residents didn't know everyone and were more likely to turn a blind eye to the activities of others.

It could be, also, that others had seen Gwen's father, but hadn't spoken of it because nobody had questioned them. If Gruffydd had been conducting a proper investigation, he would have interviewed all of the servants and castle residents. But he wasn't, for reasons Gwen still didn't understand. Gwen herself had tried, but few people were willing to talk to her about the murder.

Gwen lay back down on the pallet and gazed upwards to the shelf above her head, though she couldn't see it in the darkness. All things considered, Saran was right. Gwen preferred being a bard's daughter to the daughter of a murderer.

7

The next morning, Gwen slept later than she intended. It was already dawn by the time she awoke. She rolled up the pallet on which she'd been sleeping and hurried out of the hut. In the middle of the night, during the long hours when she wasn't sleeping, she'd come to the decision that she should bring what Edain had discovered to Gruffydd. Perhaps her information could spark him into movement. Despite his lack of action, she trusted him more than she did Robert or Cadfael. Maybe he'd at least be willing to listen.

But before Gwen was half way down the path towards the kitchen, Saran waylaid her. "I heard that you have been trying to help your father."

Gwen swallowed hard. "Yes."

Saran studied her. "And? How does it feel?"

Gwen didn't hesitate. "Terrifying. But not so much as the thought of my father being hung for murder."

Saran nodded. "I spoke with Gruffydd about the potion yesterday, and now I have something to show you."

"Something good?" Gwen said.

"Perhaps." Saran directed Gwen to a corner of the kitchen garden. A shovel rested against the chin-high wall that sheltered the plants from the wind that blew around the castle most days of the year.

Saran pointed at a hole in the ground. "I noticed that the shovel was missing when I checked my tools this morning, and then saw that the earth had been disturbed here. I'm surprised you didn't hear someone digging in the middle of the night."

"I was certainly awake for enough of it." Gwen touched the handle of the shovel, glad that Saran was so careful with her possessions, even if it made Gwen nervous to be anywhere near her things.

When Gwen had asked permission to use the herbalist's hut for music practice, Saran had given her a fierce look. She'd assented, but not before threatening Gwen with bodily harm if she moved, damaged, or otherwise touched the huts' contents in any way. Gwen's initial laughter had died in her throat when she realized that Saran wasn't jesting.

Gwen crouched to look at what Saran had unearthed: two lengths of linen cloth, wadded into balls and stuffed together in a shallow hole. Carefully, Gwen pinched the corner of one of the pieces and lifted it. Loose soil had adhered in places to the pus and blood, which had soaked through the cloth.

"The blood hasn't dried," Saran said. "I would say that whoever buried these, did so just a few hours ago."

"Someone at the castle has an injury which they want to hide," Gwen said, "or they would have come to you."

"I want to say these belong to our murderer," Saran said. "But I don't see how he could have been injured so severely in garroting Collen. Collen didn't even have skin under his nails where he might have scratched at the man."

Gwen hadn't realized that Saran had examined the body so thoroughly. "And yet—" she said.

Saran's brow furrowed. "And yet if he had nothing to fear, why not wash them, or burn them? Why risk their discovery?"

"Where would a man do that without being seen?" Gwen said. "In the great hall? It's always full. Someone would notice, just as someone would wonder about a man washing cloths at the well when it's icy cold outside."

Gwen glanced up at the herbalist, prepared to thank her for her help, when an image of Gwalchmai tuning his lyre last night came to her in a flash. She could have throttled herself for being so blind and stupid.

Saran touched Gwen's shoulder. "You know something. I can see it in your face."

"Lord Cadfael should see these," Gwen said. "I won't say more until I've spoken to Gruffydd."

"Lord Cadfael, Gruffydd, and Cadoc are leading a hunting party this morning in celebration of Cadoc's birth day." Saran checked the sky. "They should be leaving soon."

At that moment, the rear door to the keep, beyond the kitchen garden wall, slammed open. Gwalchmai bounded down the steps. "Gwen! You must come! Sir Gruffydd is bringing Father before Lord Cadfael right now!"

"What?" Gwen dropped the cloth she was holding back into the hole. "I thought he was going to wait until tomorrow!"

"Lord Cadfael is sentencing him today," Gwalchmai said. "That's what Cadoc told me."

Gwen took off running towards the door to the keep, the hem of her skirt clenched in both hands to free her legs, but then she changed course halfway to Gwalchmai and headed towards Saran's hut. She burst into the workshop, grabbed a clay dish, and dashed back to the hole Saran had discovered. Carefully, Gwen removed both lengths of cloth and placed them in the dish. Then she ran back towards the keep, collecting an open-mouth Gwalchmai on the way.

As she pushed through the door, two of Gruffydd's men urged Meilyr across the expanse of wooden floor towards the dais where Robert, Lord Cadfael's steward, waited.

"Father!" Gwalchmai had both hands to the sides of his head, as if by blocking his ears, he could stop the sentencing from happening.

Gwen turned on him. "Stay with Saran. You shouldn't watch this."

"But Gwen—"

Gwen grabbed his arm. "Please, Gwalchmai. This isn't for your eyes. I will stand with Father and support him."

Gwalchmai stared at Gwen, his mouth working, but then he closed it and obeyed her, as he'd obeyed her in the pantry, turning on a heel and going back outside. Saran met him at the bottom of the stairs.

"Please, Saran—" Gwen said.

Saran nodded and put her arm around Gwalchmai's shoulders to direct him towards the kitchen. The servants there would welcome him, and feed him, and by the time he finished eating, this would be over.

Dreading what was to come, but unable to see a path forward that didn't go through this moment, Gwen walked to stand beside Meilyr, her knees shaking. She was glad that her long skirt hid the trembling and she clenched the clay dish she had brought. She had accumulated some knowledge, and had some evidence that might indicate that her father had no involvement in Collen's murder. But mostly what she'd discovered led only to more questions, ones for which she didn't yet have answers.

Robert had cleared the hall except for Gruffydd and a dozen men of the garrison, plus Eva and Denis, both of whom had a vested interest in Lord Cadfael's decision. The couple stood in the corner by the door. Where all the other visitors to the castle had gone, Gwen didn't know, although she could hear the muster of men in the courtyard, preparing to ride out on the coming hunt.

"Girl," her father said as Gwen took her place to his right, "go away."

"No," Gwen said. "I need to hear what Robert and Lord Cadfael have to say. And you need someone to stand with you."

An expression identical to the one that Gwalchmai had just given her crossed Meilyr's face, but he swallowed down his objections without further comment and turned to face Robert. Then, Lord Cadfael entered the hall from the stairwell that came down from the upper rooms. The table that normally sat on the dais had been moved to one side. A single chair rested in a central location and Cadfael claimed it. His hands clasped behind his back, Cadoc took his place just to the right of his father's chair as he often did.

The room settled into silence. Cadfael flicked a finger at Gruffydd, who brought Meilyr to stand ten paces from him. Then Gruffydd pressed down on Meilyr's shoulder to force him onto his knees.

"Of what is this man accused?" Lord Cadfael's voice rang throughout the hall. Everyone knew of what Meilyr was accused, of course, but this was a formal setting, before the lord and judge of the castle, and the traditions had to be observed.

"Of murder, my lord," Robert said. "He was found next to the body of the man, Collen, trader and merchant. The murder weapon was found beside the body and belongs to the accused." Robert held up the harp string.

Meilyr didn't look at either Cadfael or Robert, and instead stared down at his hands.

"And what say you, Meilyr ap Brydydd?" Lord Cadfael said. "Did you do this deed?"

Meilyr shook his head, still not looking up. "No, my lord. I did not."

"Is there a man, here, who will speak for you?" Cadfael said.

More silence. Then Gwen stepped forward. "I would speak for my father, my lord."

Cadfael's eyes narrowed.

"My father does not have a son who has come of age to speak for him, so it falls to me." Gwen kept her eyes lowered and her tone courteous.

"Although it is unusual for a woman to speak in the hall, I grant your wish. What have you to say?" Cadfael said.

Gwen's head came up. "My lord, first, I would like to ask Lord Robert about the coins that Collen left in his keeping."

All of the men in the hall went rigid. Gruffydd had been standing behind her father, who was still on his knees, and now leaned in so he could speak low in Gwen's ear. "What coins?"

Gwen didn't answer. She gazed fixedly at Lord Cadfael, who kept his eyes on hers for a long moment. The nature of Welsh law was such that a defendant not only had a right to a defender, but had a right to ask questions of his accuser. Cadfael turned to his steward. "Robert?"

Robert stood a little way to Cadfael's left, opposite and more forward from Cadoc's position. "What—what coins?" Robert said.

"I know about the coins that Collen gave you for safekeeping, my lord." Gwen refused to back down or look away from the men in front of her. "You cannot keep them."

Robert's face flushed bright red. "Are you accusing me—?"

"You are accusing my father of something he did not do," Gwen said. "If you expect him to tell the truth, you must tell it also."

"Gwen is right, my lord Cadfael. You should listen to her." Denis strode towards the dais. Gwen turned so that she could see him approach. While she was terrified by her forwardness, his face showed interest and even ... amusement. "Collen told me that he had left three gold coins in Lord Robert's keeping. When I asked him about them after Collen's death, Robert claimed no knowledge of them."

Robert was sputtering. "I have no idea what you—"

"I can prove it, my lord." From his pocket, Denis pulled out a tiny book, no more than a finger's length high and wide. He opened it to a page and held it out to Cadfael.

"Collen kept very careful records of everything he bought, sold, or did."

Lord Cadfael eyed the page, and then Robert. Cadfael studied the steward for a long moment and then surged to his feet. He swung a finger to indicate the entire hall. "Clear the room! Now!"

Stunned silence followed that order, but then Gruffydd put his heels together and bowed. "Yes, my lord."

"But my father—"

Cadfael cut Gwen off with a glare. "Except for you. You stay!"

The two men who guarded Meilyr got him to his feet. Gwen remained in the middle of the floor, her hands still clenched around her clay pot. She kept her head slightly bowed while the room emptied, not sure of what had happened—or why—or what might happen next. A moment later, only Gwen, Gruffydd, Robert, Cadoc, and Cadfael remained.

Cadfael settled back into his chair. "Now," he said. "I want to know what's really going on in my castle."

Nobody answered him.

Lord Cadfael lifted his chin to his steward. "Robert, I know the truth now. Speak to me of the coins."

Robert's jaw clenched. "I have them, my lord. I understand that the possession of them gives me motive for killing Collen, but I did not kill him."

Gwen bit her lip. She didn't want to insert herself into the lords' dispute, but there was no help for it, not with what she had discovered—and remembered. "My lord, there is an easy way to determine the truth. Lord Robert should remove his gloves."

"What?" Gruffydd, Cadfael, and Cadoc spoke in unison.

"The man who murdered Collen has wounded hands," Gwen said.

Cadfael snorted his disbelief. "How would you know that?"

"I was remiss in not realizing this earlier, for it would have exonerated my father instantly," Gwen said. "No man, no matter how strong or able, could garrote another man with a harp string and not mark his palms and fingers. The strings are very sharp and will cut an unwary person if he is not careful. My father wears thin gloves when he strings his harp. Think of the damage the string must have done to the killer, who wound it around his hands and killed Collen with it."

Gruffydd glanced at the bloody harp string Robert had set on a side table. "Can you show us?"

Gwen slipped a second coil of string from her pocket and straightened it. She'd been carrying it around since yesterday, just as a reminder of what she had to do. It was two feet in length, thin and generally unbreakable except when stretched tight on her father's harp. Gruffydd took the string from Gwen and held it between two fingers. It bowed and bounced as he wiggled it.

"Imagine grasping the ends, coiling them around your hands, and garroting a struggling man with it," Gwen said.

Robert had been watching their exchange carefully, his shoulders tensed. He hesitated another heartbeat, and then with quick jerks, loosened the fingers of both gloves, pulled them off, and dropped them onto the wooden planks of the hall. "There!" He held out both hands to Gruffydd and Gwen, and then turned on his heel to show Cadfael.

"The murderer could have worn gloves," Cadoc said. "Your father remains the most likely suspect for this very reason. He must have known what you have just told us."

"That is true, my lord, except ..." Gwen took in a deep breath and let it out. "My lord, may I approach?"

Cadfael raised his eyebrows, but then nodded. Gwen walked forward, holding out the dish with the bloody rags inside. "Saran found these in the garden this morning."

The men inspected the linen with distaste. Robert sneered as he picked up one corner of a rag and held it up. "Someone is in pain."

"Nobody has come to Saran for healing?" Gruffydd said.

"No, my lord." Gwen eased out a breath. It seemed Gruffydd was becoming something of an ally, which was going to make this easier. "As Lord Cadoc said, my father would have known that he had to wear gloves to wield the harp string, and yet none were found in the pantry."

"So what do you propose?" Cadfael said. "That we inspect the hands of every man in the castle? It's an absurd thought."

Gwen didn't think it absurd at all, but his certainty made her hesitate. "Perhaps Collen's wife could be questioned—"

Lord Cadfael cut her off. "Eva did not kill her husband."

Gwen knew that he was right, given her appraisal of Eva's hands the night before, and that she was a small woman. "I know that, my lord, but *someone* did. Don't you want to discover who that is?"

Cadfael's brow furrowed. "I dislike your impertinence, young lady." He tapped a finger on the arm of his chair as he gazed at her.

Gwen swallowed. "Did Saran confirm what I said about the manner in which she believes my father was dosed?"

Cadfael continued his tapping. "She did."

"Coupled with the mead he consumed, the potion would have ensured that my father had no memory of the events of the night at all," Gwen said.

"We have no other suspect, my lord," Robert said. "We can't just release Meilyr. It will make you look weak."

Gwen didn't care in the slightest how Cadfael looked, though of course she didn't dare say so.

Gruffydd stirred. "I have a suggestion, my lord."

Cadfael glanced at his captain. "Yes?"

"We should use Meilyr to lay a trap," Gruffydd said.

Cadoc spoke from behind his father's chair. "What kind of trap?" He leaned forward, his eyes on Gruffydd. It was just the kind of thing to appeal to a fourteen year old boy.

"You threatened Meilyr with hanging earlier," Gruffydd said. "The whole castle knows of it. I propose that we announce that Meilyr is guilty as charged and destined to be hanged in the morning."

"What—?" Gwen stared at Gruffydd, aghast.

Cadfael ignored Gwen. "Go on."

"Instead of being hanged, however, what if Meilyr dies in the night? The murderer would feel himself safe. With Meilyr convicted and out of the way, he could come to Saran for healing."

Cadfael fingered his chin as he thought, his eyes on a point above Gwen's head.

"If this doesn't work, you wouldn't—he wouldn't really kill him—" Gwen could barely get the words out.

"Of course not, Gwen," Gruffydd said.

"It would be a ruse, to draw the real murderer out." Cadoc turned to Gwen. "Have you mentioned the issue of the murderer's hands to anyone but us?"

"No, my lord," Gwen said, "not even to Saran, though she is the one who found these rags."

"If we behaved as if the matter were settled, it would allow Meilyr to sing in the hall for my birth day celebration tonight," Cadoc said.

Gwen blanched. An hour ago, every man in the room had seemed set on hanging her father at the first opportunity, and now they wanted him to sing.

"It might work," Cadfael finally said.

Robert glanced at his lord quickly and then turned away, running his hand through his hair. Gwen forced her eyes away from the steward and towards Cadoc, who was grinning, unaware of the silent communication and tension in his elders. A moment ago, Cadfael had given Robert a look that had been *knowing*. What was going on here? Robert might be innocent of murder, but she was beginning to believe there was more to

this than she had so far uncovered.

8

The hunting party returned at dusk in good spirits, having killed two deer for the feast. The kitchens had been prepared for failure, which meant that the celebration of Cadoc's birth day would now be doubly fine. The scent of roasted meat wafted across the courtyard with every gust of the wind. Gwen could smell it, even from inside her father's cell.

"All of this is my own fault, Gwen." Meilyr paced back and forth in front of his daughter.

"How can you say that?" Earlier, Gwen had related to him what had happened in the great hall, and Gruffydd's plan for him. Her father had been opposed to it at first, but in the intervening hours, had come around, willing now to play his part.

"I should never have brought us here in the first place," he said. "We should have stayed in Powys."

"Lord Thomas asked us to stay," Gwen said. "Why did we leave?"

"Because we'd been there for months already and Collen wanted me to come here. He promised to make it worth my while," Meilyr said. "He and Lord Cadfael."

"And now Collen is dead," Gwen said.

Meilyr nodded. "Though it was mighty convenient for Cadfael to find me guilty of murder. If he really had hung me, he would have owed me—or rather you and Gwalchmai—nothing. No wonder he preferred that punishment to requiring me to make the payment of *galanas* to Eva."

"Wait, Father—what are you saying?" Gwen kept stumbling over ideas that were new to her. "You're telling me that Cadfael cannot pay what he owes us for the winter?"

Gwen's family had never lacked food and shelter, for all that they'd wandered Wales since they'd left Gwynedd. Their voices were their entry into any home, high or low. But Cadfael was a lord. How could he not have the resources to compensate her father for their services?

"Why else would Robert keep the three gold coins that belonged to Collen?" Meilyr said. "He has always been upright in his dealings with me in the past. It is very unlike him to be dishonest. The only thing that makes sense to me is that once Collen was dead, Lord Cadfael ordered him to keep the coins secret."

"Did he really think Collen wouldn't have told Denis of them?" Gwen said.

Meilyr stopped in mid-stride and turned to his daughter. "Have you learned nothing these last few days? How much more likely is it that Collen acquired the coins and kept that information from his partner and his wife."

Gwen's shoulders fell. "Oh."

Meilyr rolled his eyes. "For all that you have a sudden propensity for uncovering truth in others, you need to be less trusting."

Gwen bit her lip, hating to be told she'd been naïve, but knowing her father was right. "You're saying that Cadfael's plan was to keep the coins, remain silent, and hang you."

"Cadfael would have been the richer for it," Meilyr said.

"But neither Cadfael nor Robert knew of Collen's little book," Gwen said. "They counted on their station to protect them from Denis."

"What they didn't count on was you defending me, upending their plans." Meilyr shot Gwen a look that she wanted to interpret as pleased or proud, but it was an expression he so rarely directed at her, she wasn't sure. "In the course of an hour, Cadfael loses both the gold coins and—with the evidence turning in my favor—still has to pay me for our time at Carreg Cennen."

Gwen shook her head. "And we can't say a single word about it, for fear he changes his mind and really hangs you. Robert is going to announce that you are guilty at the start of the evening meal."

The power Cadfael wielded left Gwen with a sick feeling in her stomach. She'd always known that good and bad lords existed in Wales, but she'd grown up in a stable home, in the household of the old King Gruffydd of Gwynedd. Even their departure from Aberffraw, even the ending of her marriage hopes with Gareth, hadn't opened her eyes to the ways of the world as much as this accusation of murder.

"I would almost rather have paid Eva the *galanas* and been done with it," Meilyr said.

"Don't say that!" Gwen said. "How can you say that? You'd let a murderer go free?"

"I would accept it, but the admittance of guilt would hang over my head, and thus yours and Gwalchmai's, for the rest of our lives," Meilyr said. "I could not do that to you."

Gwen swallowed. Her father had to be thinking primarily of Gwalchmai, but he had included her in his calculations too. She wasn't used to him doing that. "Could you have paid her even without Cadfael's contribution?" Gwen said.

"It would have beggared us," Meilyr said.

"We've been poor before." Gwen thought of that first year after they'd left Gwynedd. Her father had been proud and had not wanted to accept a place in any castle but that of a mighty lord. In the end, they'd spent the winter at Aberystwyth, the seat of Prince Cadwaladr, King Owain Gwynedd's brother. That was how she'd met Gareth, since he'd been a man-at-arms in Cadwaladr's retinue. Because of Gareth, Gwen couldn't regret father's choice of residence, but it had solidified the enmity between him and King Owain. It wasn't a good thing to be on the bad side of a king, especially as a bard who had to sing for his supper.

"Not as poor as this would have made us," Meilyr said. "I'm offended that Gruffydd gave me so little credit for my ability to think. He and Cadfael must have mocked me for being such an imbecile to have murdered a man with my own harp string and then stayed with the body. What did they take me for?"

"Men see what they want to see." In the past few days, Gwen had learned that, at least.

Gwalchmai appeared in the doorway. "It's time, Father."

"Are you ready?" Meilyr directed a sharp gaze at Gwen. "We never practiced our song."

"It can't be helped now," Gwen said.

"Let's go." Gwalchmai led the way out of the cell, bouncing on his toes. He loved to sing—loved everything about it, from the sound of his voice, to the study of meter and rhyme, to the performance itself—and it was that characteristic as much as his magical voice that would make him a great bard. If the people of Deheubarth didn't know it already, they would after tonight.

This evening, Gwen's family had diverged from their usual custom of eating the meal in the hall and rising at the end to sing, or even playing throughout the meal, in favor of a more formal ceremony. Gwen hadn't eaten at all, though she'd seen Gwalchmai well fed in the kitchens and brought her father's tray to him herself.

The hall quieted as Gwalchmai, Gwen, and Meilyr filed through the main doorway, not because they had entered the room, but because Robert had risen to his feet at the same time.

"Lord Cadfael did not want to sully his son's birth day with unpleasant tasks, but it has already been sullied," Robert said. "You all know of the death of Collen, the merchant and trader ... I must announce that Lord Cadfael has found Meilyr, the bard, guilty of his murder. He will be hanged in the morning."

A wave of confused noise rose and fell throughout the hall: horror, maybe, shock even, and surprise that the Welsh tradition of *galanas* would be overlooked in favor of the Norman sentence of death.

Cadfael sat with a finger to his lips, observing the reactions of his guests. Cadoc had moved to stand to the right of his father's chair, as he had stood during Meilyr's sentencing. Gwen noted when his gaze sharpened on Eva and Denis, who sat in the middle of a far table. Eva had turned on the bench, so her back was to Denis and she faced towards the room. Denis wore a look of bemusement and took a sip of wine.

As she looked at Meilyr, however, Eva's face had transformed from that of an innocent beauty to a vengeful matron.

Gwen stared at her, and then flicked her attention away, just as Eva trained her eyes on Gwen and Gwalchmai. By the time Gwen dared to raise her head, Eva had faced back to Denis who was pouring her a cup of wine from a flagon.

Robert had remained standing. "As a last request, Meilyr asks your pardon, if not your forgiveness, and joins us in the celebration of Cadoc's birth day."

At Robert's nod, Meilyr led Gwen and Gwalchmai up the center aisle to the dais. A stir ran around the room. To the eyes of everyone there, Meilyr was a dead man walking. She knew her father was hating every step he took, hating to be the object of scorn and ridicule—and pity. It gave a poignancy to the moment that Gwen herself didn't feel. She was too caught up in worrying about the aftermath of the singing, and whether they really would be able to ride away from Carreg Cennen in one piece.

When they reached the high table, Gwlachmai and Meilyr bowed and Gwen curtseyed.

"Bard," Cadfael said.

Even with the unveiling of Robert's deceit, Gwen was pleased to see no animosity in Cadfael's eyes as he looked at them. From beside his father, Cadoc's face was lit from within. He had become a man today, shot a deer with his own arrow and then slit its throat, and from now on would take up his duties as his father's right hand man. Gwen hoped that he had learned something from these past few days and would not follow his father's duplicitous example.

"My lord," Meilyr said, speaking formally. "We have prepared a song in honor of Lord Cadoc's birthday. Do we have your permission to sing it?"

"Yes," Cadfael said.

The three singers moved to one side of the dais and then turned to face the audience. Gwen allowed her focus to blur, so she couldn't see individual faces. On a happier day, she might have enjoyed the guests' expressions, but not tonight.

Gwalchmai began with a long solo, and then Meilyr and Gwen joined him. The song was a complicated one, in which Gwen and her father traded melodies while Gwalchmai's soprano soared above the rest. Gwen, Gwalchmai, and Meilyr held the last note in perfect harmony.

And then Meilyr clutched his chest, staggered, and fell to the floor.

The hall erupted once again in noise and confusion.

Instantly, Cadfael was on his feet, Cadoc beside him, their faces a caricature of shock. Then Gwen caught Cadfael's eye and lifted one shoulder, just slightly. Cadfael's mouth snapped shut. With identically blank expressions, both men lowered themselves back into their chairs. Gwen was sorry to ruin Cadoc's birth day feast, but since he was in on the deception, if not the exact moment it would occur, she couldn't feel too bad. Meilyr and Gwen had felt that everyone's surprise would be more authentic if the two of them chose the manner of Meilyr's demise, rather than leaving it to the dark hours of the morning.

Saran pushed her way through the crowd. "Let me past! I can help him."

The onlookers gave way, though Gwen heard an older man mutter something about it being "better this way." Saran fell to her knees beside Meilyr and Gwen leaned over her father, to block them from the general view of the hall. Meilyr was trying to lie still and unmoving on his own but once Saran held a cloth under his nose and he breathed in the scent—only one breath but it was enough—he relaxed completely and his head flopped to one side.

Saran slipped the cloth back into its pouch and sat back on her heels. Gruffydd, who had been crouching near Meilyr's head, his hands resting on his knees, straightened. That motion quieted the hall and Gruffydd held up one hand. "He is dead."

Gwalchmai had pressed his back to the wall, watching the proceedings with wide eyes. Gwen went to him and pulled him into her arms. "It's all right, Gwalchmai."

He'd known of the plan too, but even so, the shock of its implementation had a trickle of tears running down each cheek. Gwen kissed the top of his head and looked out at the other diners, most of whom had settled back into their seats. Gruffydd already had his men working to carry Meilyr from the hall.

Cadoc appeared on Gwen's left. "You saw Eva's reaction to Robert's announcement?"

"I did," Gwen said.

"Did we miss something there?" Cadoc said.

Gwen glanced at him. He was tall for fourteen, with a man's voice, and his tone was that of a man too. He would make a fine heir to Cadfael if he kept his head. "Eva brought my father to the pantry the night Collen died."

"She what?" Cadoc spoke louder than he should have and several heads turned in their direction. He moderated his tone. "Why didn't you say so before?"

"I only found out about it a few hours before my father's sentencing. And since I had no more evidence than a maidservant's middle-of-the-night vision, I thought it best to leave it as it was," Gwen said. "I had your agreement that my father didn't murder Collen. Eva played a part, surely, but she didn't murder her husband."

Cadoc pursed his lips. "Perhaps not."

"She is too small and slight to subdue a man twice her size. But did she help it along?" Gwen nodded. "I think so."

"I will keep an eye on Denis," Cadoc said. "He's worn gloves ever since he arrived."

"Given Eva's anger, that he is involved is a natural assumption," Gwen said.

"I, for one, would like to know the reason behind her anger," Cadoc said.

"I would say *galanas*, or the lack thereof," Gwen said.

"You may be right." Cadoc eyed Gwen. "If your hunch is correct, we should know more soon."

"And if I'm wrong," Gwen said. "Then my father will have a miraculous recovery." She took a step towards the door, bringing Gwalchmai along with her. "I should be with him, my lord."

"Of course."

"Best wishes on your coming of age," Gwen said, because she did truly wish him well.

"Thank you. I will be sure to remember you the next time we have a murder at Carreg Cennen. My father should call upon you to solve it." Cadoc gave her a slight bow before turning away, leaving Gwen speechless, staring after him.

9

Gwen tucked a blanket all around her father and leaned in to kiss his forehead. He lay on the table in an alcove in the chapel. In a larger, more well-appointed castle, the chapel would have had a room set aside specifically for housing the dead, but not here.

A door banged and Gwen spun around to see Gruffydd marching towards her. He'd let in a waft of cold air and a swirl of the snow that had begun to fall after the midnight hour had passed. Gruffydd came to a halt beside Meilyr's body. "How is he?"

"Asleep," Gwen said. "He's barely breathing, but Saran says that's normal. As we progress towards morning, he should come awake. He'll be disoriented then."

"Can you leave him?" Gruffydd said.

"I—" Gwen paused and narrowed her eyes at the captain of the guard. "Why?"

Gruffydd took Gwen's arm. "He'll be fine. Come with me."

"Where are you taking me?" Gwen trotted beside Gruffydd, trying to keep up. He wasn't exactly dragging her out of the chapel, but his grip on her arm was firm.

"Cadoc told me what he saw in the hall this evening, and of your conversation with him."

"You mean Eva?" Gwen said, no closer to understanding why Gruffydd was hauling her halfway across the castle in the middle of the night. Unusually, given the hour, the courtyard was lit as if it were day and so many boot prints had marked the new snow that hers barely made an impression.

They reached the barbican that guarded the castle and went through it. Built primarily in wood, with an accompanying wooden palisade, Carreg Cennen Castle primarily relied on its position on the top of a mountain for defense. The castle dominated the landscape with a spectacular view of the countryside for miles around. At the same time, Cadfael had done what he could to bolster the defenses.

The castle was protected by a fortified gateway, beyond which a series of bridges crossed several deep pits. Each had been built so that anyone seeking entry to Carreg

Cennen had to walk along a narrow walkway with no railings to reach the entrance. At any time, the bridges overlying the pits could be drawn away from their supports, creating an insurmountable chasm-like barrier.

Gruffydd took Gwen to the second bridge, stopped in front of the guard standing in the middle of it, and pointed into the ditch below. The snow-covered body of a woman lay at the bottom, her torso jammed on a pointed stick, one of many that filled the hole and were designed to kill anyone who fell into it.

"Sweet Mary," Gwen said. "It's Eva."

Gruffydd tipped his head to the two men-at-arms who had climbed into the pit to retrieve the body. "Bring her up."

"Who found her?" Gwen said.

"At the change of duty, one of the men-at-arms spotted her from the tower," Gruffydd said.

"How could he even see her in the dark and the snow?"

"He has eagle eyes," Gruffydd said. "But it wasn't her he spotted as much as the remains of footprints in the snow leading from the barbican to the bridge, and then stopping."

Gwen couldn't take her eyes off the gruesome scene. "What a horrible way to die."

Gruffydd took Gwen's shoulders and turned her around so she faced him instead of Eva. "Her satchel lies beside her. It looks as if she was leaving Carreg Cennen and slipped on her way across the bridge."

"It *looks*?" Gwen said. "She had to pass through the gatehouse to get here. Who saw her leave?"

Gruffydd looked away, his jaw working. "No one."

"How is that possible?" Gwen glanced past him to the barbican. The heavy wooden door was open. "Wasn't anybody guarding the gate?"

"The main gate was closed at nightfall, but the wicket gate beside it can be opened at need. The guard on duty was drunk and doesn't remember anything," Gruffydd said.

"Was the wicket gate found locked, even after she passed through it?" Gwen said.

"Yes."

"Then—"

Gruffydd understood where Gwen was going without her having to voice her question. "Then who closed it behind her? I don't know."

"My lord!"

Gruffydd turned towards one of his soldiers, who handed him the strap to Eva's satchel. He opened it and allowed Gwen to peer into its depths with him. "Is that what I think it is?" he said.

"I think so." Gwen reached inside and removed a small, stoppered vial. She held it up. "The potion, do you think?"

"It seems likely. I will inquire of Saran in the morning," Gruffydd said, taking it from Gwen.

"Were there two sets of footprints leading to the bridge?" Gwen said.

"The guard didn't notice," Gruffydd said. "By the time one of the men woke me, the snow was too muddled to tell."

"Someone could have pushed Eva off the bridge," Gwen said.

"*Someone*," Gruffydd said. The word came out a growl. "Our murderer is still here at Carreg Cennen. Let's hope my plan works."

But by noon the next day, it didn't seem like it was going to. Fortunately the weather prevented all but the hardiest from leaving the castle—and none left before Gruffydd had inspected their hands. Gwen sat alone on a bench at one of the far tables, feeling morose, while Cadoc picked at a trencher of food, mostly uneaten.

Half an hour earlier, they'd been entertained by Denis berating Robert at his carelessness in letting Eva leave the castle under such severe weather conditions. The merchant was only appeased by the production of the three gold coins he'd coveted. That his unmarked hands had been bare for the first time since he'd arrived only added to the low mood of the watchers.

Several men-at-arms were seated around the room, one of whom was asleep with his head on arms folded on the table. From the bleariness in Cadoc's eyes, he'd had more to drink than he should have to celebrate his birth day.

"Come this way, Ifan." Saran's voice came through the open doorway to the great hall. "I left my medicine bag in here last night after dealing with Meilyr."

Gwen looked up as Ifan and Saran entered the hall by the rear door.

"I guess the bard got what he deserved," Ifan said, following closely on Saran's heels.

Saran glanced at Gwen and then away again before Ifan noticed. Gwen sat frozen to her bench, fearful that she'd draw Ifan's attention by any word or movement. Saran and Ifan headed towards the opposite wall.

"Did he?" Saran said. "Does any man deserve to die?"

Her heart in her mouth, Gwen rose to her feet and drifted along in Ifan's wake. She came to a halt close to the dais and twenty feet away from Ifan. She put out one hand

and rested on it the high table. As she'd stopped directly in front of Cadoc, he lifted his head. Gwen fisted her hand. Gareth had told her that men used their hands to speak to one another during battle, when a sound might give away their position. A fisted hand meant. "Danger!" It was the only signal Gwen could remember.

Cadoc either understood what she was trying to tell him, or could sense that something was happening just by the tension in Gwen's body. He rose to his feet just as Ifan sat on the bench that Gwen and Gwalchmai had occupied the other night. Gwen couldn't breathe as Saran removed Ifan's padded gloves and unwrapped the cloths with which Ifan had bound his hands, revealing bloody gashes across his palms and on his fingers.

"Why didn't you come to me sooner?" Saran said.

Ifan shrugged. "I thought they would heal."

"How did this happen?" Saran held each of his hands in hers, gazing down at the wounds.

Gwen had eyes only for Saran and Ifan, but Cadoc must have signaled to someone to find Gruffydd and his father, because suddenly the captain of the garrison was on one side of Ifan and Cadfael came to lean against the wall behind him, out of Ifan's view.

"Forking hay for the horses." Ifan blanched at the sight of Gruffydd so close to him, but continued, "It's been so cold that the blisters split. They've gotten worse over the last few days."

"Don't bother lying, Ifan. We know why you didn't seek aid," Gruffydd said.

Ifan licked his lips. "What—what do you mean?"

"You killed Collen." Gruffydd said.

All of a sudden, it was just that simple.

From her pocket, Gwen pulled the harp string she'd been carrying with her since Collen's murder. She handed it to Gruffydd who laid it across Ifan's hands. The servant flinched as it touched him.

"That would do it," Gruffydd said.

"*Why* did you murder Collen?" Cadoc said.

Ifan still hadn't answered, whether to deny or admit what he'd done, but with the same flash of inspiration, Gwen thought she knew. "It was Eva."

Ifan's jaw clenched as he stared down at his hands, and then his face twisted in hatred. "Eva." He spat onto the rush mats on the floor.

"She told you that you would inherit the cart, didn't she?" Gwen said. "She suggested that she might even share the *galanas* with you, if only you would do this one thing for her."

"Did she kiss you, too?" Gruffydd said. "Make you other promises you believed?"

Ifan's teeth clenched and unclenched. "She swore— she *swore* that—" Ifan broke off and pressed his lips together.

Gruffydd crouched in front of Ifan. "She swore that it would be easily done, is that it? And that the two of you would be together afterwards?"

Where anger might have closed Ifan's tongue, Gruffydd's gentle voice persuaded. Ifan must have been bursting to speak of what he'd done for days, and now that it seemed he was caught ... "She was the one to lure Collen to the pantry with promises of renewing their affections. It was dark when he entered and I surprised him. We grappled with one another, but I was the stronger, and there was the harp string ... it was over quickly. I slipped away before Eva brought Meilyr in shortly afterwards."

"How could you do it? He was like a father to you," Gwen said.

Ifan shot a glare in her direction. "He was no father. I was his *slave*!"

Gwen recoiled at the venom in his voice, recalling what Wyn had told her about Collen's penchant for beatings.

"I stayed with that cart, I did what I was told, for ten years. Did I ever receive a kind word from him? You say he treated me like a son, but what son is tied forever to a cart, even in the dead of winter?"

"And you got nothing for it," Saran said.

"*Nothing.*" Ifan spat again.

"Why the harp string?" Gruffydd said. "Why blame Meilyr?"

Now a sulky expression came over Ifan's face. "Eva chose him. She said that he had money and nobody liked him anyway. With the boy's voice coming into its own, Cadfael could let the father go."

All the blood left Gwen's face but she struggled not to take offense on her father's behalf. "You didn't think that wrapping a thin iron string around your hands might hurt them?"

Ifan's chin fell and he shook his head. Gwen supposed that he didn't have many thoughts in his head but resentment. Eva had given him hope for the future when he'd had none.

"Two murders, then," Cadoc said. "You committed two murders in my father's house."

Ifan had been gazing at his wounded fingers and at first didn't seem to hear Cadoc. Then he looked up . "What? You mean—?" Ifan stared at Cadoc and then swung his head from side to side, *no, no, no.* "I didn't kill Eva."

Disbelief coiled tangibly in the air around him.

"I didn't!" Ifan said. "Yes, we fought after dinner when I learned that not only would there be no *galanas*, but that with Meilyr dead, she had no more use for me. But I went back to my cart. I didn't know what else to do. It was because I was sleeping there as always that I heard Eva come out of the keep."

"She was leaving Carreg Cennen?" Gwen said.

"She dosed the guard at the wicket gate right then and there," Ifan said. "One whiff of her potion and he was on the ground, just as Meilyr had been. She slipped away immediately after. I ran to the gate. I called to her—well, whispered really. Even so, I startled her. She spun around, but with the ice and snow on the bridge ..."

"She slipped," Gruffydd said.

Ifan rubbed at his temples with his fingers. Tears had begun to leak from his eyes. "I never meant for any of this to happen."

Gruffydd gazed down at the wayward assassin. "They never do."

10

Meilyr stuffed a nightshirt into his satchel. "I suppose I should thank you."

He spoke so softly, Gwen wasn't sure she'd heard him properly. She stood stiffly, watching her father put the rest of his spare clothing into the pack before she realized what he was doing. "We're leaving?"

"Heading north."

"Why?" And then Gwen swallowed, already knowing why. She gazed down at her feet.

"It's best that we leave," Meilyr said. "Lord Cadfael told me as much just now. We'll find a place to stay for the rest of the winter. Gwalchmai's reputation will precede us."

Gwen nodded. "Did Cadfael pay you?"

"He paid some, though not all, of what he owes. He swore if we come back in the summer, he will have the full amount."

"But we won't be coming back," Gwen said.

"No."

"I'm sure Cadfael is counting on that," Gwen said.

Her father cleared his throat. "Gruffydd spoke to me too."

Gwen's head came up. "What did he say?"

"He asked that I thank you for your help, and he wished you the best."

"Oh." Gwen bent her head again. She could feel her father's gaze on her but she didn't meet his eyes.

"Lord Cadfael would have opposed a request from Gruffydd to marry you," Meilyr said.

Gwen bit her lip. She toed a crack in the floorboards and didn't speak.

"It wouldn't do for his captain to marry a woman such as you," Meilyr said. "You couldn't really have thought he would approve of it."

"What do you mean, *such as I*?"

"Gwen." Her father's voice held amusement, rather than chastisement, which almost irked her more. "You are outspoken. You defended me before Lord Cadfael himself. You can't think that Lord Cadfael would want to see you in his hall every evening? Or that Gruffydd would be proud of such a wife?"

Gwen took in a deep breath and let it out. "No. Of course not. You're right."

Meilyr nodded and continued with his packing.

"So we keep moving?" Gwen said. "Following the music?"

Gwen had resolved to follow Saran's advice and not wish her life away, but at the same time, a tendril of hope curled inside at the thought of heading north again. Gareth had gone north. Maybe he was out there somewhere. Maybe she really *would* see him again someday.

Meilyr allowed himself a small smile as he tied the strings on his pack. "You are a bard's daughter, Gwen. This is what we do."

The End

Thank you for reading *The Bard's Daughter*. All of the books in the *Gareth and Gwen Medieval Mysteries* are available at any bookstore. For more information about dark age and medieval Wales, please see my web page: www.sarahwoodbury.com

A Historical Note ...

For *The Bard's Daughter*, I have drawn upon some very basic principles of Welsh law, though I have simplified the process for the purpose of story-telling. Welsh law was one of the founding pillars of Welsh society, and was codified by a King Hywel Dda, around 950 AD. Rarely was death a penalty for a crime, and it was instituted more often for theft than for murder.

Later on, with the arrival of the Normans, Welsh law proved to be a rallying point for the Welsh resistance against Norman rule. The Normans objected to many of the laws (paying money instead of a sentence of death for various crimes, the relatively high status given to women, the ability to divorce, etc.), but the most contentious of all were Welsh rights of inheritance. In Wales, illegitimate sons and legitimate ones were treated identically before the law, which allowed Prince Hywel of Gwynedd, Gwen's friend, to inherit equally with any of his father's legitimate sons.

For crimes such as murder and theft, the Welsh relied upon a system of courts, overseen by landowners and lords, to determine guilt. Often, this determination was based upon *compurgation*, whereby witnesses testified to the truthfulness of the accused.

For the most part, Welsh law was in force in the parts of Wales under Welsh control until the death Llywelyn ap Gruffydd in 1282, when Norman law replaced Welsh criminal law. Welsh law continued to be used for civil cases until the annexation of Wales into England in the 16th century.

In addition, there really was a bard named Meilyr, who sang for King Gruffydd of Gwynedd. In turn, his son, Gwalchmai, became one of the most revered bards of the twelfth century, exactly as Meilyr hoped.

Continue reading for the beginning of *The Good Knight*, the first novel in the series of Gareth and Gwen Medieval Mysteries:

The Good Knight

1

August, 1143 AD

Gwynedd (North Wales)

"Look at you, girl."

Gwen's father, Meilyr, tsked under his breath and brought his borrowed horse closer to her side of the path. He'd been out of sorts since early morning when he'd found his horse lame and King Anarawd and his company of soldiers had left the castle without them, refusing to wait for Meilyr to find a replacement mount. Anarawd's men-at-arms would have provided Meilyr with the fine escort he coveted.

"You'll have no cause for complaint once we reach Owain Gwynedd's court." A breeze wafted over Gwen's face and she closed her eyes, letting her pony find his own way for a moment. "I won't embarrass you at the wedding."

"If you cared more for your appearance, you would have been married yourself years ago and given me grandchildren long since."

Gwen opened her eyes, her forehead wrinkling in annoyance. "And whose fault is it that I'm unmarried?" Her fingers flexed about the reins but she forced herself to relax. Her present appearance was her own doing, even if her father found it intolerable. In her bag, she had fine clothes and ribbons to weave through her hair, but saw no point in sullying any of them on the long journey to Aber Castle.

King Owain Gwynedd's daughter was due to marry King Anarawd in three days' time. Owain Gwynedd had invited Gwen, her father, and her almost twelve-year old brother, Gwalchmai, to furnish the entertainment for the event, provided King Owain and her father could bridge the six years of animosity and silence that separated them. Meilyr had sung for King Owain's father, Gruffydd; he'd practically raised King Owain's son, Hywel. But six years was six years. No wonder her father's temper was short.

Even so, she couldn't let her father's comments go. Responsibility for the fact that she had no husband rested firmly on his shoulders. "Who refused the contract?"

"Rhys was a rapscallion and a laze-about," Meilyr said.

And you weren't about to give up your housekeeper, maidservant, cook, and child-minder to just anyone, were you?

But instead of speaking, Gwen bit her tongue and kept her thoughts to herself. She'd said it once and received a slap to her face. Many nights she'd lain quiet beside her younger brother, regretting that she hadn't defied her father and stayed with Rhys. They could have eloped; in seven years, their marriage would have been as legal as any other. But her father was right and Gwen wasn't too proud to admit it: Rhys *had* been a laze-about. She wouldn't have been happy with him. Rhys' father had almost cried when Meilyr had refused Rhys' offer. It wasn't only daughters who were sometimes hard to sell.

"Father!" Gwalchmai brought their cart to a halt. "Come look at this!"

"What now?" Meilyr said. "We'll have to spend the night at Caerhun at present rate. You know how important it is not to keep King Owain waiting."

"But Father!" Gwalchmai leapt from the cart and ran forward.

"He's serious." Gwen urged her pony after him, passing the cart, and then abruptly reined in beside her brother. *"Mary, Mother of God..."*

A slight rise and sudden dip in the path ahead had hidden the carnage until they were upon it. Twenty men and an equal number of horses lay dead in the road, their bodies contorted and their blood soaking the brown earth. Gwalchmai bent forward and retched into the grass beside the road. Gwen's stomach threatened to undo her too, but she fought the bile down and dismounted to wrap her arms around her brother.

Meilyr reined in beside his children. "Stay back."

Gwen glanced at her father and then back to the scene, noticing for the first time a man kneeling among the wreckage, one hand to a dead man's chest and the other resting on the hilt of his sheathed sword. The man straightened and Gwen's breath caught in her throat.

Gareth.

He'd cropped his dark brown hair shorter than when she'd known him, but his blue eyes still reached into the core of her. Her heart beat a little faster as she drank him in. Five years ago, Gareth had been a man-at-arms in the service of Prince Cadwaladr, King Owain Gwynedd's brother. Gareth and Gwen had become friends, and then more than friends, but before he could ask her father for her hand, Gareth had a falling out with Prince Cadwaladr. In the end, Gareth hadn't been able to persuade Meilyr that he could support her despite his lack of station.

Gwen was so focused on Gareth that she wasn't aware of the other men among them—live ones—until they approached her family. A half dozen converged on them at the same time. One caught her upper arm in a tight grip. Another grabbed Meilyr's bridle. "Who are you?" the soldier said.

Meilyr stood in the stirrups and pointed a finger at Gareth. "Tell them who I am!"

Gareth came forward, his eyes flicking from Meilyr to Gwalchmai to Gwen. He was broader in the shoulders, too, than she remembered.

"They are friends," Gareth said. "Release them."

And to Gwen's astonishment, the man-at-arms who held her obeyed Gareth. Could it be that in the years since she'd last seen him, Gareth had regained something of what he'd lost?

Gareth halted by Meilyr's horse. "I was sent from Aber to meet King Anarawd and escort him through Gwynedd. He wasn't even due to arrive at Dolwyddelan Castle until today, but ..." He gestured to the men on the ground. "Clearly, we were too late."

Gwen looked past Gareth to the murdered men in the road.

"Turn away, Gwen," Gareth said.

But Gwen couldn't. The blood—on the dead men, on the ground, on the knees of Gareth's breeches—mesmerized her. The men here had been *slaughtered.* Her skin twitched at the hate in the air. "You mean King Anarawd is—is—is among them?"

"The King is dead," Gareth said.

———————

The Good Knight is available wherever ebooks are sold.

About the Author

With two historian parents, Sarah couldn't help but develop an interest in the past. She went on to get more than enough education herself (in anthropology) and began writing fiction when the stories in her head overflowed and demanded she let them out. While her ancestry is Welsh, she only visited Wales for the first time while in college. She has been in love with the country, language, and people ever since. She even convinced her husband to give all four of their children Welsh names.

She makes her home in Oregon.

www.sarahwoodbury.com

Made in the USA
Middletown, DE
16 March 2018